MIDNIGHT MAGIC

MIDNIGHT
MAGIC

SCHOLASTIC INC.

New York   Toronto   London   Auckland   Sydney
Mexico City   New Delhi   Hong Kong

ISBN 0-590-36036-1

24 23 22 21 20 19 18 17 16   9/0

Printed in the U.S.A.   40

First Scholastic club printing, March 2000

The text type was set in 13.5/17 M Bell.
The display type was set in Trajan and Inscription.
Cover art by Laurel Long
Book design by Marijka Kostiw

for Katie

chapter 1

In 1491, in the Kingdom of Pergamontio, there lived a twelve-year-old boy by the name of Fabrizio. He was the sole servant of Mangus the Magician.

One sweltering summer eve, near midnight, a violent storm broke over the city where Fabrizio lived. Lightning splintered the inky darkness. Thunder rumbled like siege guns. The falling rain fell with the sound of a million hissing snakes.

Dirty faced, scrawny, and shaggy haired, the boy was sitting in the dry front hall of his master's ancient timbered house, wearing an old, long-sleeved tunic with a belt made from a piece of frayed rope. His cloth boots were hand-me-downs of hand-me-downs.

Close at hand was a lantern that burned a flame no bigger than a button. There was also a cudgel with which he was supposed to beat away anyone who tried to enter the house. But as far as Fabrizio was concerned, the most important thing before him was a tattered pack of tarot cards. These cards, he believed, could fashion the future. Since he could envision no life for himself other than as a servant, it was his master's fate he wished to shape.

When the great cathedral bells rang twelve times, Fabrizio, knowing midnight was the best time to cast the cards, reached for the deck. But now that the hour had come, he was so nervous, his trembling fingers could barely square the pack of cards, much less shuffle them.

When he finally managed to do so, he took a deep breath, brushed the hair back from his eyes, and turned over the first card. It was

THE MAGICIAN

Fabrizio smiled. Who else could the card represent but Mangus?

He turned the second card. It was

THE SERVANT

This time, Fabrizio laughed. No doubt as to who *that* card represented. That his master's fate included him was exactly his desire.

Quickly, he laid out the next six cards:

THE CASTELLO   THE KING   THE GHOST

THE PRINCESS   THE TUTOR   THE QUEEN

Fabrizio frowned. He had hoped for something better.

It all looked too much like Mangus's past life. Nonetheless, the boy readied the last card, the one that would determine his master's ultimate fate.

Eyes shut, praying to see *Riches*, Fabrizio turned over the ninth and final card. When he opened his eyes and saw that the card was

DEATH

he gasped.

Even as he did, a crash of lightning shook the house. Simultaneously, an explosive pounding erupted on the front door. The summons came so suddenly, and at such an appallingly awful moment, the tarot cards spurted from his hands like a geyser.

Terribly frightened, Fabrizio scooped up the cards, jammed them into his pocket, groped for the cudgel and lantern, and jumped to his feet.

The knocking grew more insistent.

"I'm coming!" he cried as he hurried down the hallway. "I'm coming!"

By the time Fabrizio reached the front door, he decided to be cautious. No telling who — or what — was on the other side. Had he not just cast the Death card?

"Who's there?" he called.

"A message from the castello!" came a shouted reply.

The castello! Death itself would have been more welcome. Fabrizio's first thought was to run to his master and give warning. After all, it was only ten months since Mangus, arrested and brought to trial in that same castello, had, under threat of torture, confessed and repented of being a magician. Though Mangus's life had been spared at the last moment by King Claudio, he remained under house arrest and was watched constantly. Not allowed to even step outside, Mangus had agreed to shun all who came to his door.

So although the magician's house was in the heart of the city, the old man and his wife — her name was Sophia — had lived like hermits since the trial. For all they knew, the rest of the world had ceased to be. Only Fabrizio was allowed to venture forth for such necessities as food.

At one time Mangus had three servants. When he went on trial, two had fled, not wishing to serve a man who more than likely was going to be burned to death at the stake for wizardry. Fabrizio felt otherwise. Having lost both his parents when he was young, he was overjoyed when the City Corporation bound him over to Mangus. In those days the magician was a rich and honored citizen. Only when he was arrested did wealth and respect evaporate. Fabrizio, however, was not going to abandon the man who had been like a father to him.

"Open up!" came a cry from beyond the door.

Hands shaking, Fabrizio pulled back the iron bolt, cracked open the door, and peeked out. By the feeble glimmer of his lantern light he saw a soldier standing in the swirling rain. The man's black cloak whipped in the wind like an angry raven's wings.

"A message for Mangus the Magician," the soldier shouted above the storm.

"Signore!" Fabrizio called, reciting the response he had been instructed to give to all who came to the door: "My master, Mangus of Pergamontio, no longer practices magic! Under the loving protection of King Claudio, thirteenth of that name, he has seen the error of his ways and has repented! Magic is an evil!"

"Evil or not," the soldier returned over the roaring storm, "it's urgent he come to the door!"

Fabrizio gave another practiced reply. "Signore!" he cried. "If you wish to engage my master with anything concerning his former, sinful ways, he will not see you!"

At this, the soldier shifted his position slightly, enough so Fabrizio could look upon the narrow, water-soaked street. Another flash of lightning revealed a carriage. Large and black with four ebony horses in its traces, it suggested great wealth. But the most meaningful thing Fabrizio saw was that the insignia on the carriage door — by which he might have discovered on whose authority the visit was being made — had been hidden by a piece of cloth. It made Fabrizio recall the old saying "Bad news always hides its face."

"Signore," he cried, "don't you understand? My orders are to let no one in! Master Mangus has renounced his past! He wants nothing to do with those who try to lure him back to sinfulness!"

The solider wiped rain from his face. "Well spoken, cur," he mocked. "And, might I add, well performed."

"It's true!" the boy exclaimed, and made an attempt to shut the door.

The soldier kicked the door back open with his booted foot. Then he drew a scroll of parchment from beneath his cape and, attempting to shield it from the rain with his free hand, thrust it at Fabrizio. "Take this to your master," he commanded. "It's from King Claudio. Count Scarazoni himself awaits in the carriage to escort you."

"Count Scarazoni!" Fabrizio cried. Not only was Scarazoni the king's closest adviser, most people believed he was the real power in the kingdom. Fabrizio knew him best as the principal tormentor of Mangus at his trial.

As Fabrizio took the parchment, he said, "Signore, would you care to wait inside?

"In a magician's house? Are you mad?"

"Whatever you say, Signore!"

Slamming the door shut, Fabrizio all but burst into tears, convinced that, by casting the tarot cards, he had brought on his master's doom. With leaden feet, he went off to search for him.

chapter 2

Mangus's house — three levels high — was squeezed between two other old buildings, like an exclamation point. On each floor were two rooms with little windows of thick glass that allowed but a smidgen of light to slip through. Warped oak-beamed ceilings were low, floors uneven. Every wall was stained and blackened by decades of hearth fires and the soil of close living. The few pieces of furniture — several chairs, a table, beds, two clothing cabinets as well as chests — were crude and heavy. The only ornaments were religious articles and rugs that hung upon the walls. The first were there to remind the family of their duty. The second helped to keep the weather out.

Mangus's study was on the first floor, in the back. A glimmer of candlelight seeped from beneath the door. Knowing that Mangus might nonetheless be asleep over his books, Fabrizio knocked loudly.

"Who is it?" Mangus's voice replied.

"Master, it's me! Fabrizio!"

"Go away, boy. I'm reading."

"Master, Count Scarazoni is at our door!"

A sharp intake of breath was followed by the words "Come in!"

Fabrizio pushed the heavy door open.

The master's study, like all the rooms in the house, was not just small, it was dark and smelled of old wax, old ink, old age. Stuffed with parchment manuscripts, as well as scrolls, it included a few volumes of the new kind of books that were printed, not written out by hand as they were meant to be. But then, as Fabrizio knew, the household had fallen very low.

Two large chests containing magical apparatus sat against the wall. Since the trial they had been kept tightly closed. Filling the room's center was a table littered with papers and books as well as a human skull that held a candle. The candle — all but guttered — cast twin beams of feeble light through the skull's eye sockets. Behind the table was Mangus.

Rather small in stature, with stooped shoulders and tired eyes, the man had aged considerably since his trial. His beard was long and white. His receding hair made it advisable to wear a cap with flaps to keep his ears warm. His lips were set in a thin, grim line and were all but blue. His eyes revealed great weariness.

Mangus was dressed in a multilayered robe of dark brown over which lay a faded Turkish shawl. Wool-lined slippers covered his feet. Though it was summer, embers glowed in the floor pot designed to hold heat. Half gloves were on his fine, delicate hands. But then, no matter how warm, Mangus complained of cold.

"Did you say Scarazoni is at the door?" the old man asked, his voice trembling even as the storm rumbled outside.

Fabrizio came forward. "Master," he whispered, "he's in a carriage. When I opened our door a soldier was there. The first thing he said was, 'A message for Mangus the Magician.'"

Mangus blanched. "Are you sure he used those words?"

"I'm certain, Master. He gave me this." Fabrizio held up the parchment. Seeking to lighten the mood, he added, "Do you wish me to make it disappear, Master?" So saying, the boy took the parchment, crumpled it in his hands, then made a swirling motion with his right hand. The parchment vanished.

Mangus leaped up, aghast. "Fabrizio!" he cried. "How many times have I told you? No more tricks! People will turn against you as they have me. Give me the message."

Chagrined, Fabrizio removed the parchment from his tunic sleeve, where he had slipped it. Mangus took it and resumed his seat behind the table. Sliding the skull closer, he began to read. After a moment he pressed his hands against his temples, an image of pain and despair that reminded Fabrizio of one of the gargoyles on the cathedral roof.

"Very well," Mangus said with resignation. "I have been summoned to the castello for a consultation with the king."

"Master," Fabrizio offered, "have you thought of escaping?"

The old man looked up.

Fabrizio slipped around the table, pushed aside a wall rug, and peeked out through a tiny window. Lightning flashed.

"What do you see?" Mangus whispered.

"Soldiers."

Mangus shook his head. "Count Scarazoni," he said with resignation, "always plans well."

"But —"

"Fabrizio, return to the door and tell the soldier I'll attend the count shortly. Then inform your mistress that I've been summoned. I'll want to say good-bye."

"Must you go, Master?" Fabrizio asked.

"Fabrizio," Mangus replied wearily, "in the old days I was famous for making things disappear. If I could do tricks as well as you do I'd begin with myself. But I have no choice. Yes, I must go." A tear trickled down his withered cheek.

Fabrizio flung himself upon his knees. "Forgive me, Master," he cried. "This is all my fault!"

Mangus gazed down with astonishment. "What do you mean?"

The boy reached into his pocket and produced the tarot cards. "This afternoon," he blurted out, "I took these from your trunk. When midnight struck I cast your future. I wanted it to be good. Instead, I turned the Death card. And the moment I did, Master, Scarazoni appeared at the door. Oh, Master," the boy cried, "you know my entire desire is to help you. Forgive me."

Mangus shook his head sadly. "Fabrizio, tarot cards are nothing but ignorant superstition. I never used them except to do simple tricks and sleight of hand. While you were wrong to take them, there's absolutely no connection between what you did and what has happened. It's a dismal coincidence."

Fabrizio remained on his knees. "Please, Master, show you forgive me by letting me go with you. I'll try to make amends by being helpful."

Mangus smiled grimly. "Ah, Fabrizio, how could you help me in the castello?"

"Master, you know what they say: 'Though the old people of the world have yet to find a way to make a person invisible, one can be young. It often amounts to the same thing.'"

Mangus gazed upon the boy with affectionate puzzlement. "Fabrizio," he said, "where do you learn these things you say?"

"The rich have schools and books, Master. The poor have eyes and ears." He lifted his hands in supplication. "Master, let me go so I'll know you've excused my folly."

"Fabrizio," Mangus said gravely, "if you come with me, you must act with utter respect, do as I tell you, and" — he lifted a finger in warning — "absolutely *no* tricks of magic."

"Master, as they say, 'I'll be as ignorant as a worm and obedient as a donkey.' Just let me help you."

"Though your life may be in danger?"

"Even though."

Mangus studied the boy. Then he made the sign of the cross over his own heart. "The Lord knows I'll need all the help I can get. Very well. You may come with me."

Fabrizio hurried back to the front door, where the soldier was waiting. "Signore," the boy cried through the storm, "my master — who is trembling in his eagerness to attend the king — will be with you in moments."

"Tell him to hurry," the soldier said. "I'm soaked."

"Do you wish to come in out of the storm, Signore?"

The soldier shook his head vehemently. "A wet man does not fear the rain," he cried as thunder boomed above.

"Leave it to a soldier to know the best hiding places!" Fabrizio retorted. Retreating into the house, he dashed up the dark, narrow stairs to the room where Signora Sophia slept.

"Signora!" he called, rapping hard upon her door. "Wake up! Master's been called to the castello."

Signora Sophia jumped out of her curtained bed and opened her door. She was a comely, gray-haired lady with a kind face worn with care. "God have mercy!" she cried. "Will they never leave the poor man alone! What has happened now?" she demanded.

"Signora, King Claudio has summoned Master for a consultation."

"About what?"

"Master doesn't know."

Sophia wrung her hands. "He'll need help. But they'll never let me join him."

"Signora, the master asked me to go with him."

"Oh, Fabrizio," Sophia cried, embracing the boy, "heaven will reward you. But you must be prepared for the worst." She ran back into her room and returned with a few old coins. "Use them wisely," she said, and rushed down the steps.

Fabrizio shoved the coins into his pocket, then ran to his cramped attic quarters. From beneath his straw pallet, he retrieved a few magic trick items he'd hidden away. He stowed them in his pocket, too.

By the open front door Mangus and his wife hugged each other. "God keep you," she whispered.

"And you."

"Magician!" the soldier called impatiently. "Don't keep the count waiting!"

Mangus turned. "Signore," he said in a quavering voice, "I am at your service."

As they went out into the storm, lightning flashed in the dark sky.

chapter 3

Mangus, with help, stepped into the carriage. Fabrizio followed. As they took their places on one of the two facing benches, the door shut behind them.

Inside, all was dim and steamy, the only light coming from a scrawny candle in a wall socket. Its yellow flame fluttered like a frightened butterfly, just enough to illuminate the face of Count Scarazoni.

A slim man of middle age, the count had a lean face, with dark eyebrows that swept over his eyes like an iron bar. His chin was shaped by a short, pointed beard. On his hands were gloves of black leather, faced with yellow cuttings. From his hip hung a dagger of Toledo steel.

No sooner did Mangus seat himself than Scarazoni banged on the carriage ceiling. With a lurch, they began to move, jolting over the street stones. The armed soldiers trotted behind.

As the carriage rumbled on — rocking and swaying — no one spoke. When Fabrizio dared to look up, he saw that the count's cold eyes were fixed on Mangus.

The old man sat with his head bent, eyes closed. Now and again he rubbed his gloved fingers, as though attempting to create fire with thin sticks.

"My lord," Mangus said at last, "with permission, may I know what the subject is about that the king wishes to consult?"

"Your wizardry," the count said curtly.

"My lord," Mangus said momentarily, "you know I practice no such thing."

"The king believes you do," Scarazoni replied.

"Am I to be tried again? Placed in prison? Tortured?"

Scarazoni said nothing.

Mangus, his voice quivering, said, "My lord, surely I may know if I am about to be put to death."

In reply, Scarazoni drew his dagger and used

its tip to snuff out the candle, plunging the carriage into darkness.

Mangus let forth a little groan, made the sign of the cross, and shut his eyes again.

Distressed, Fabrizio tried to look outside. But the carriage's window shutters had been drawn, making it impossible for him to see anything. It did not matter. He knew they were going to the castello.

Though born and raised in the city, Fabrizio had never been to the castello, which sat atop the steep hills and cast a shadow over the municipality. It was not just the place where the king, his family, and court lived; it contained the power of life and death over every citizen in the kingdom. Many a soul had been brought there never to be seen again.

The structure was bigger than any building in the city, larger even than the cathedral. Fabrizio had little doubt it was the grandest building in the world.

In shape, the castello was roughly rectangular. The longest wall faced west and rose two hundred feet. At each corner stood a turret of some additional one hundred and fifty feet. Along the front and back walls were two other turrets, evenly spaced. At the base of these towers were dungeons, where — as every citizen of Pergamontio knew — lay prisoners' bones.

The castello's walls, fashioned from dark volcanic rock, were topped off with the jagged teeth of a crenellated parapet. Night and day, citizens could observe sentries pacing along these ramparts, their silver helmets and spears glinting.

The walls contained holes through which arrows could be shot. Here and again cannon muzzles thrust out their metallic snouts, ready to spit fire like dragon heads.

Beyond this bulwark the castello's many storerooms were reputed to be so full, its wells so deep, it had never given way to siege. If it were ever to fall — or so it was said — it could only be from rottenness within.

But as Fabrizio approached the castello, he was thinking not of wars or plots but of the great danger in which he had placed his master by casting the tarot cards. He made a private vow: Though it could cost him his life, he would do everything and anything to help the magician.

After lumbering up the city's steep terrain by threading through the maze of narrow streets, the carriage came to a halt.

"You must not be seen," Scarazoni barked. "Pull up your hood."

Fabrizio reached behind Mangus and helped lift the cowl and settle it over his master's eyes, obscuring his face.

The carriage door opened. First to climb out was Scarazoni. Next came Fabrizio, the better to help his master. The moment they alighted, soldiers surrounded them.

Though wet and windy in the city below, it was stormier upon the castello's outer bailey. Lightning sparked. Thunder drummed. Wet winds beat down like heavy hammers.

"This way," Scarazoni cried, guiding the way to the gatehouse steps. These steps, built into the southern wall, were made of stone and so narrow that they had to go in single file. A misstep meant a plunge to death.

Reaching the top, they continued along a wooden platform set over a moat flooded with foul water. Once beyond the platform they made a sharp left turn and continued over a lowered drawbridge. Halfway across, a voice challenged from above, "What's the password?"

The demand came from the gatehouse, a wooden chamber built partly over the entry bridge. The room contained a murder-hole, so called because it had a trapdoor that, opening directly over the bridge, allowed soldiers to shoot unwanted intruders as they approached the gates.

"Long life to Claudio!" one of Scarazoni's party cried.

"Pass!"

The portcullis — the castello's heavy gate — rose slowly, metal chains shrieking in protest.

It was only Count Scarazoni, Mangus, and Fabrizio who went forward. Behind them the portcullis dropped with a *crash*. They passed through a tunnel in the thick stone wall before moving into a hallway, the inner bailey.

The hall was vast. The dank air stank of rot and mold. Burning oil lamps — giving off as much smoke as flame — were stuck in walls. The flickering light caused shadows to dance wildly upon the walls like maddened imps. It made Fabrizio think they had been swallowed, Jonah-like, into the belly of an enormous beast.

To the left and right of the hall — three levels one atop the other — were rooms with balconies. Soldiers lived on one side; kitchen, stable, and court staff were on the other. Though Fabrizio was reminded of a beehive, not a soul was in sight.

They crossed the length of the hall, not stopping until they faced an entrance screened by elaborate panels of carved wood. There they halted. New soldiers appeared.

Scarazoni turned to Mangus. "They will search you for weapons," he announced.

When the search was complete — nothing was found — Scarazoni stalked behind the screen.

Mangus, quite wet, absentmindedly pulled back the hood that hid his face. No sooner did he do so than some of the soldiers began to study him intensely.

One of them, a hulking, fierce fellow with a heavy crossbow upon his back, abruptly pointed at Mangus and barked, "You there! I know you. You're Mangus. The magician!"

Mangus shook his head. "No more," he said.

"But you were once — weren't you?" the soldier persisted.

"Yes, Signore, I was," Mangus replied, his voice contrite.

A young soldier pointed at Fabrizio. "And the boy?" he jeered.

"My servant," Mangus returned.

The soldier made a gruntlike laugh. "I would have thought a magician like you could just wave his hands and the house would be clean."

The soldier's words stung Fabrizio. How dare

they mock his master! Furious, he reached into his pocket and pulled out one of the coins Signora Sophia had given him. He held it up.

Puzzled, the soldiers stared at him.

Mangus, realizing what Fabrizio was doing, cried, "Fabrizio! Don't!"

Too late. Fabrizio made a simple pass, wiping his left hand over his right hand, which held the coin. As he did, he deftly palmed the coin into his left hand, creating the illusion that it had disappeared.

The soldiers gasped with astonishment. As Fabrizio replaced Mangus's hood over his master's face, he smiled.

The next moment, Count Scarazoni returned from behind the screen. "Mangus!" he called. "King Claudio the Thirteenth bids you enter."

chapter 4

Leaving the soldiers behind, Count Scarazoni led Mangus and Fabrizio through the screened entrance into another hall. Though not as large as the one from which they had just come, this hall had just as high a ceiling.

No matter where Fabrizio looked, he saw fine furniture, rich tapestries, elegant emblems, elaborate wood carvings. Vibrant colors and gold were everywhere. Upon the walls hung flags, swords, and fighting shields, some stained with blood. The wealth and power of it all astonished him.

But instead of the multitude of courtiers, clerics, and servants he expected to see, only four people were present. They stood upon a slightly raised platform at the far end of the room. Most prominent was King Claudio the Thirteenth, absolute ruler of the Kingdom of Pergamontio. He was seated on a massive chair with lion claws carved into each arm head.

Fabrizio had seen the king many times in the lower city amidst important processions. Then, dressed magnificently, surrounded by people of the court as well as by a fierce personal guard, he had appeared very powerful.

Close-up, however, he was seen to be a short, heavy, square-faced man of middling years. His skin was coarse, his nose bulbous, his lips — surrounded by a heavy, curling beard of gray — were thick and frowning. His wet, nervous eyes were fixed upon Mangus, while his fat fingers drummed on the arms of his chair.

The open greatcoat he wore was fur-lined, the dark, flat hat upon his head cocked low. Attached to a loose belt was a dagger, hilt encrusted with jewels. Chains of heavy gold were about his thick neck. Rings glittered on all his fingers.

Seated on the king's right was Queen Jovanna. Fabrizio had seen her less often than the king. Having been born and raised in another kingdom, almost a hundred miles away, she was a foreigner and thus not overly trusted by the Pergamontian populace.

Though her chair was set lower than her husband's, it was easy to see she was the taller of the two. Quite thin, she wore a long, loose-fitting, fur-lined velvet coat over a dark blue gown. A stiff lace ruff encircled her neck like a yoke, while a modest golden cap made her face appear small and intense.

Standing behind the queen — one hand on her shoulder — was her daughter, the princess Teresina. Fabrizio had seen her only during one religious procession in the lower city.

Fabrizio knew little about her. Though not nearly as tall as her mother, she closely resembled the queen. They were even dressed the same. But the stillness of the princess's features, her rigid stance, and her unwavering gaze made Fabrizio think of a statue: no flesh, blood, or — for that matter — heart. Mangus had told him the princess had faithfully attended his trial for wizardry, watching him intently throughout. Fabrizio hardly knew if it was proper for him to look at her or not.

She did have an elder brother, Prince Lorenzo, heir to Pergamontio's royal throne. He was not there.

Another man was standing off to one side, his posture humble. Stunted in stature, dressed in long black robes and a black academic cap, he stared at Mangus with frightened eyes.

"My lord," Count Scarazoni called when he came within six feet of the platform, "I bring you Mangus the Magician."

Mangus bowed low. Fabrizio did a crude imitation.

The king looked about. "Is the door secure?" he asked.

"It is, my lord," Scarazoni replied.

"No one saw him arrive?"

"He was hooded."

The king fidgeted on his chair. He tried to stare at Mangus, but his eyes, full of fear, kept turning away. "Well, Mangus," he said at last, even as he clasped and unclasped his hands, "I trust you are well."

Mangus bowed again. "As well as can be expected, my lord," he said, "from a man who has gathered his years and his lessons in pain."

"You are still alive, are you not?" Count Scarazoni cut in sharply.

The king winced. So did Fabrizio.

"By your mercy, my lord," Mangus acknowledged meekly.

"There were many who wanted to put you to the stake, Mangus," Scarazoni went on. "They would have rejoiced to see your heart turned into a lump of glowing coal. If you dance with the Devil, your feet will feel the heat."

"My lord," Mangus replied piteously, "for six days I lay in your dungeon awaiting execution before your mercy saved me."

Scarazoni smiled. "I'm pleased you know whence your good fortune comes."

"My lord," Mangus said, "I am forever in your debt."

Fabrizio saw him shudder slightly.

The king shifted uncomfortably on his chair. "I am pleased to hear you say that, Mangus. Since you are a magician —"

"My lord!" Mangus exclaimed. "I must protest!"

The boldness of the objection so startled the king that his hand dropped to the hilt of his dagger. Fabrizio wanted to run away.

"Protest?" the king returned with indignation. "How so?"

"To practice the dark arts is a great sin, my lord," Mangus proclaimed with all the energy he could muster. "I abhor such acts with my heart and soul. My lord, I was never more than a *pretender*, a trickster, a charlatan. Every bit of magic I ever did was the work of mechanics and sleight of hand. As you well know, my lord, my magic — my *so-called* magic — was entertainment for the gullible. A thing of theater, nothing more than the means of earning bread for my wife and home when I could not live by thought alone. My lord, I beseech you, humbly, to believe me. I am not now — nor have I ever been — a dabbler in ways of evil. I seek to be a good Christian. My profession is a philosopher."

Fabrizio, impressed that Mangus had the courage to speak out so, stole an admiring glance at his master.

The king shrank back into his chair. "But, Mangus," he said, "you know magic and the netherworld from which it climbs."

"My lord, with permission, believe me. *I have no such knowledge.*"

Count Scarazoni spoke out. "At your trial, Mangus, you were found guilty of brewing the stews of Satan. You confessed it all."

"My lord count," Mangus replied bitterly, "to be found guilty by those whose only evidence is fear is but a judgment on their own fears."

Scarazoni's dark eyebrows seemed to stiffen into metal. "Do not," he cried out, "forget it was I who convinced the king to lend you mercy!"

Such was the force of the count's words that Fabrizio took a step back.

The king's little eyes shifted nervously. He wrung his hands. "Count Scarazoni speaks the truth, Mangus," he said. "It was I — acting upon the advice of my chief adviser" — he nodded to Scarazoni — "who spared your life. You say you are in my debt. Well, then, good. It is time to repay that loan."

"My lord, my only desire is to help you in any way reason will allow," Mangus returned with yet another bow.

The king attempted to sit up with something suggesting authority. His effort, however, was undermined by anxious glances at his wife, his daughter, and toward the count.

Then he leaned out of his chair and spoke. "Mangus," he said, with a catch in his voice, "it's not your *reason* we are in need of. It's your wizardry! Mangus, in all my kingdom, it's you" — the king's voice turned to pleading — "and only you who can free my daughter from a terrifying ghost!"

chapter 5

Fabrizio was so frightened, his legs shook.

When Mangus found his voice, it was barely audible. "My lord, if there is, as you say, a ghost, since I do not believe in them, I . . . I can only fail at what you ask me to do."

"Well, yes," the count interjected. "We understand your desire to say so. There are laws against magic. Our people fear it. It's our duty to protect them."

Mangus bowed his head.

"Well, now," the king said impatiently, "let us get on with this. The business must be resolved in haste."

"Mangus," Scarazoni interjected, "what you are about to hear must be known *only* to those present. This is a state secret. Pay heed, there are traitors and enemies everywhere. We have reason to believe there are spies in the castello."

Momentarily, the king worried his hands. Then he spoke: "Mangus, it was Princess Teresina who has seen this thing. She —" He turned to his daughter. "Teresina, child, tell your tale to the magician. Just as you related it to us."

The princess seemed not to have heard. During all that had been said, she had appeared statuelike to Fabrizio. Not so much as blinking an eye, it looked as if she were in a trance. "It began," she said in a flat, unemotional voice, "some twenty-one days ago. The ghost appeared like an indistinct radiance along the north wall not far from my chambers."

As she spoke, the queen watched her intently. So did the third man who was there. Even Fabrizio, putting aside his fears, could not help but gaze at her.

"I was going to the latrine and did not wish to bother my lady-in-waiting. The time — by the cathedral bells — was near midnight. When the thing appeared, I could not believe what I was seeing. The vision was as bloodless and still as stone itself.

"When I first saw it," the princess continued,

"I reached out to touch it. Dead as the castello walls are, they, at least, ooze water that drips into drainage gutters and flows away. Such water can be touched. What I saw could not, would not, be felt. My hand passed through it."

Fabrizio's blood ran cold.

The girl went on: "Frightened, I hastened to say a prayer, then fled back to my chamber. Secure in my bed, I decided what had occurred was but a dream."

King Claudio interrupted. "That was why, Mangus, she told no one about the ghost except her wise tutor during her regular morning lessons."

The king made a gesture toward the small man in black robes who had been standing silently off to one side. At the mention of the words "wise tutor," this man darted a jittery glance at Mangus, smiled weakly, then looked away in haste.

"The wise Signore Addetto," Scarazoni said, "also believed it was no more than a dream. Though a dream of that kind was in itself worrisome, he told the princess to be more contrite in her prayers, to distribute more alms, and, above all, to be obedient to her parents."

The king took up the story. "Not only did the princess promise to try, she did as she was told.

On her own, Mangus, in the middle of the night, she goes to our private chapel and seeks guidance. She is, I assure you, a most dutiful daughter." He turned to the princess. "Go on with your story."

The girl went on. "When the ghost did not return, I thought prayer was indeed the answer. But, a few days later, I saw the apparition again. It came to me in the same place, in the same way, at the same hour."

"Mark that, Mangus," the king interrupted. "This suggests that this thing — whatever it is — knows my daughter's habits. Proceed," he said to his daughter.

"This time," the princess went on, "when I saw the ghost, its radiance had gained some human form. It throbbed like a living heart. Most dreadful of all, it reached out to me."

Fabrizio, all but feeling the ghostly hand on him, trembled.

"Terrified," the princess said, "I ran back to my chambers and woke my lady-in-waiting and informed her of what I had seen. She hastened with me back to the place. She saw it, too. But we told no one.

"Two days later," the girl continued, "I observed the ghost a third time. It came to me in

the same place. I hastened to my mother" —
here, the girl looked to the queen — "and told
her what I had seen."

"Queen Jovanna," the king said, "you will
please continue."

The queen sat straighter. "I tried to console
my weeping daughter," she said. "By way of
comfort I told her I would go to see for myself.
Accordingly, I went to the spot where she said
the ghost appeared. I saw nothing at all.

"In the morning the princess asked me if I had
seen the vision. I told her I had not. But the
princess," the queen concluded, "insisted a ghost
had been there."

The king spoke next. "The queen — as was
proper — informed me of this matter. I questioned
the princess carefully. As you know, Mangus, I,
too, have some knowledge of the spirit world."

Fabrizio noted that his master was about to
say something but restrained himself.

"She told me what she had seen," the king
went on. "Naturally, I was skeptical. I encouraged the child to accept the fact that it was an
illusion, something fancied; at worst, a bad dream.

"But you see, Mangus," the king said, "I knew
the princess — no matter how she tried — still
believed in this ghost." He pounded his armrest

in frustration. "She does not tell lies, Mangus!" he cried in anguish. "I know that! And ghosts exist! I know that to be true!"

Fabrizio glanced around to see his master's reaction. To his surprise, he saw great sadness.

Count Scarazoni spoke next. "As a way of relieving the princess's anxieties, I offered to patrol the corridors outside her chambers at night for a week.

"I did so. Once, twice, the king joined me. So did wise Signore Addetto. None of us saw one thing amiss."

The king said, "There the matter rested until last night. Princess, say what you experienced then."

The princess lifted her chin. "Just past midnight I saw the ghost again. This time, it spoke to me."

"*Spoke*, my lady?" It was the first time Mangus had said anything to the princess.

"Tell Mangus what the ghost said," the king whispered hoarsely.

"The ghost insisted I go with him. To the other world."

As the princess closed her eyes — her tale done — Fabrizio felt a chill.

The king squirmed in his chair. "Mangus," he

said, "I tell you Princess Teresina does not lie. Yet neither her mother, nor Count Scarazoni, nor I saw this thing that so clearly threatens her life and soul."

Mangus cleared his throat. "My lord, with permission, may I ask a question?"

Claudio glanced at Scarazoni. The count nodded. "Permission granted," the king said.

"My lord, you say only those in this room know of this. Yet the princess made reference to her lady-in-waiting, as well as to her tutor. I see Signore Addetto is here. But the lady-in-waiting, where is she?"

Count Scarazoni smiled and said, "She has joined a nunnery and taken a sacred vow of silence."

"More blessed she," Mangus said softly. Then he said, "With permission, another question."

"Speak," the king replied.

"Your son — the prince Lorenzo — no mention of him has been made. Has he seen it?"

The king fidgeted. Count Scarazoni glared. The queen moved uneasily. The princess coughed slightly. But no one answered the question.

"Have I misspoken?" Mangus asked, aware, as was Fabrizio, of the nervousness his question provoked.

"Prince Lorenzo," the king finally replied, "is on a diplomatic mission to the pope, in Rome. He knows nothing of this."

"And no one else is aware of this matter save those in this room?" Mangus asked.

"Except for the people here," Count Scarazoni replied, "this . . . thing remains a total secret." Then he snapped, "Mangus, this business must be resolved quickly."

"How much time do I have, my lord?" Mangus asked, in such a way that Fabrizio could see how weary he was.

"A few days," the king replied.

"A few days! With permission," Mangus said, "may I ask why there is such urgency?"

"No," Scarazoni said. "You need not know. Mangus," he went on, effectively changing the subject, "it would be best if you remained confined to a room unless accompanied by myself or the king. Talk to no one without permission."

"And my servant, my lord?" Mangus inquired, gesturing to Fabrizio.

The boy darted a look up. The king glanced at him briefly, then turned to the count.

Scarazoni said, "Your boy is free to run your errands on the presumption he knows his place."

"A most loyal and obedient servant, my lord," Mangus said.

"So be it," the king said, only to lapse into silent thought. Then he said, "Mangus, your wizardry must rid us of this ghost."

Mangus sighed. "My lord, the only thing more fearful than what we know is that which we do not know."

"No excuses, Mangus," Scarazoni scolded forcefully. "Consider how fortunate it was that the king spared your life before. Now you can re-pay him for his kindness. It is your obligation to free the princess of this torment."

"And if I cannot do so, my lord?" Mangus asked softly.

The king scowled. "If you cannot?" he echoed, at a loss for a reply, though his hand fell to his dagger hilt again.

Count Scarazoni answered the question. "Mangus, if you cannot help Princess Teresina, there will be no more reason to spare your mis-erable life."

In his mind, Fabrizio saw the final tarot card.

chapter 6

Mangus — with Fabrizio at his side — was led through the castello by a silent soldier.

To the boy's surprise, the castello was no cleaner than the lower city. The stench was just as bad. Green mold clung to stone walls. Garbage was everywhere. Once, twice, three times, he saw rats scurrying by.

As for their chamber, it was meager and lit by a solitary candle. Without a window, it was close, smelling of decay. The stone floor was scattered with old rushes. The only comforts were a narrow rope bed covered with a thin wool blanket, and a clay jar of water. By way of adornment, a large, door-sized panel was affixed against one wall. Dark with age, it depicted the martyrdom of blessed Saint Stephano, pierced with a thousand arrows.

Fabrizio guided Mangus over to the bed. Exhausted, the old man sat hunched over, staring before him, eyes full of tears. Now and again he stroked his beard. "I am undone," he whispered.

Fabrizio knelt before him. "What do you mean, Master?"

"This task the king has called on me to do — to rid the princess of this . . . *thing* she calls a ghost — I cannot accomplish it."

Fabrizio chafed Mangus's hands, trying to provide some warmth. "In the morning, Master," he said, "when you have slept and have taken measure of your wits as well as Princess Teresina's visitations, you'll know what to do."

"Fabrizio," the magician said with anger, "whatever the girl observed, or thought she observed, was no ghost. There are no such things."

"Master, she saw it four times. It even spoke to her."

"She deludes herself. All these fanciful trappings to her tale," he said with scorn. "Midnight ghosts. Voices from smoke and flame. Bodies in chapels. Mark me, we shall have creaks and groans ere long. Shabby theater, all of it! As for the king "— Mangus fairly groaned — "I fear he truly believes I am a wizard.

"Oh, Fabrizio," Mangus cried with anguish, "beware the man who first condemns you for your wits, then begs you to use those wits to save him!

"In any case," the old man continued bitterly in a softer voice, "all Italy knows Scarazoni is the power here. The king is nothing."

"Master," Fabrizio said, "does Scarazoni believe you to be a sorcerer, too?"

"Of course not. A year ago popular unrest was aimed at him. He brought me to trial to distract the people. Someone to blame."

"Ah, Master," Fabrizio agreed, "it's like they say, 'If the earth is barren, blame the moon.'"

Mangus nodded sadly.

"But, Master," Fabrizio asked, "who was that other man there? He seemed very frightened of you."

"Signore Addetto? The tutor of the princess? Scarazoni's minion. A dolt."

"And why," the boy continued, "was there silence when you asked the king about Prince Lorenzo?"

"I have no idea. But this ghost —" Mangus shook his head.

"Now, Master," Fabrizio chided, gently removing his master's shoes and massaging his frigid feet, "the whole world knows there are ghosts. You, so old and wise, how can you say otherwise?"

Mangus, in a pique of frustration, pushed the boy away.

Fabrizio went sprawling, banging into the jug of water and tipping it over. The water drained away midst the floor rushes. Fabrizio looked on with dismay. "Forgive me, Master," he cried. "I'm clumsy."

"It was not your doing," Mangus said ruefully. "I lost my temper. You see what a lack of reason does."

Wanting to placate his master and get him to lie down, Fabrizio only said, "Master, whatever it is, you'll find a way to deal with it."

Mangus looked at the boy with weary eyes. "Fabrizio," he said, "you are the living proof that even someone who reads can be a fool. Very well, then, they have brought me here, a virtual prisoner. I shall have to prove there is no ghost."

"Master, you need to rest."

"True, a weary mind makes weary thoughts,"

Mangus replied, letting himself be eased down upon the bed. Once on his back, he shut his eyes, crossed himself, then folded his hands over his beard and chest.

"Is there anything else I can do for you, Master?" Fabrizio asked as he spread the thin blanket.

"At moments like these," Mangus said, "I recall the old wisdom that though time is the most valuable thing a man can have, it can buy him no more time. But I could use some water, Fabrizio," he murmured. "My mouth is dry."

Eager to be helpful, the boy said, "I'll fetch some."

"They probably have locked us in."

Fabrizio tiptoed to the door. "Master," he whispered, "it's open." He peeked beyond. A soldier lay asleep on the threshold. "Signore," Fabrizio called softly.

The soldier did not wake.

Fabrizio crept back to Mangus. "Master, there's only a sleeping guard. I'm sure I can slip by and bring some water."

"We are the perfect pair," Mangus murmured. "I am sure of nothing. You are sure of everything."

Fabrizio grinned and said, "You know what

they say, Master, 'A wise man and an ignorant man, each reveals the other.'"

Mangus sighed. "You may be ignorant, Fabrizio," the old man said, "but you are kind. And kindness is the most underrated of all human qualities."

"Master, my whole desire is to make life good for you."

"Bless you."

"I'll be back soon," Fabrizio said. "I promise." As he edged away, Mangus began to mutter prayers.

With care, Fabrizio stepped over the sleeping soldier, then shut the door behind him quietly.

He looked up and down the corridor. Other than the sleeping soldier, all was deserted. A few oil lamps, set in high wall sconces, flickered faintly. Vaulted ceilings faded into nothingness.

Fabrizio had no idea which way to go. It was as if he had stepped into a tunnel that came from nowhere and went to a similar place. Then he recalled that an old woman had once told him that when lost, he should always avoid going to the left. Accordingly, he walked to the right.

Staying as close to the stone walls as possible, he crept along the hallway. All too quickly he reached a "T." Once again he went to the right, only to come upon a flight of steps where another soldier lay sprawled asleep. Fabrizio moved around him, went down another level, turned right again, but found himself facing a blocked passage.

Retreating in the direction he had come — or thought he'd come — he looked for a sign to help him find his way. He found none, except now and again bats fluttered by, emitting high-pitched squeaks. From somewhere a dog yelped as though in pain. Other dogs joined in, followed by different sounds — groans, moans, and rasping creaks. Fearful, Fabrizio stopped. As suddenly as the sounds came, all became still. He pressed on.

More than once Fabrizio halted, certain someone loomed ahead. Each time it proved to be nothing more than a wooden statue or a stone figure set in an alcove and shrouded with dust-encrusted webs.

He passed many doors. Once, he thought he had returned to their own. Upon checking it, it proved different.

"Who goes there!" The cry was so unexpected, Fabrizio fairly leaped off the ground in terror.

A soldier sprang forward, sword extended. By his side, a dog growled and strained at its leash.

Fabrizio whirled and began to run, plunging down corridors as fast as he could.

"Halt! Stop!" came the cry. A dog began to bay. Other dogs took up the cry.

When Fabrizio saw a flight of steps, he raced down but was so breathless when he reached the bottom, he had to stop. Sides aching, he listened. When he heard nothing, he made up his mind to forget the water and get back to his master.

Though Fabrizio continued to meander, it was not long before he became so bewildered, he had to stop. He had no idea which way to go. But even as he remained in place, he gradually became aware that on the wall opposite where he had stood was a light where no light should have been. It was, moreover, gray-green, the color of decay.

Fabrizio squeezed an ear to make certain he was awake before he looked again. Sure enough, though neither lamp nor candle were close, he was seeing an illumination whose existence was distinct and separate from the walls that surrounded it. It stood — or rather floated — four feet above the ground, with a fluttering radiance that kept within a specific niche. The more Fabrizio stared at it, the more convinced he grew that the illumination contained the shape of a person. It was — Fabrizio was sure — a ghost.

chapter 7

As Fabrizio continued to stare, he began to see more within the shadowy form: a head, shoulders, hands. Then one of the hands seemed to unfold its fingers like a blooming flower. To Fabrizio's horror, it appeared to be pointing directly at him, as if accusing him of something. Then it occurred to him that the thing was pointing elsewhere. He turned. Standing behind him was Princess Teresina.

Devoid of finery, she was not unlike the girls with whom he played on the crowded, filthy city streets. She was wearing a light shift. Her feet were bare. Her face, accented by the hallway gloom, was very pale. Her eyes were round with fear. Fabrizio found it hard to know who was more spiritlike, the girl or the glow upon the wall.

"The ghost," Teresina said as though in a trance. "It's telling me to come."

Fabrizio said, "Come where?"

"To death."

"My lady," he whispered, "I don't hear a word."

"But you see it, don't you?"

"Yes, I do."

The shadowy shape grew larger, giving Fabrizio the sensation that it was moving in their direction.

"Keep it away!" Teresina implored in a quavering voice.

Fabrizio tried to drag her from the place. She would not move. Panicked, he looked over his shoulder. The thing had become even bigger.

"Don't let it take me!" Teresina cried. "Don't let it!"

Heart hammering, Fabrizio stepped forward. "Begone!" he cried, hardly knowing if he was shouting or whispering.

The light continued to enlarge. Then, as if responding to Fabrizio's command, its brightness began to fade. Within moments, it had gone. No sooner had it vanished than Teresina uttered a moan and collapsed to the ground.

Fabrizio knelt beside her. "My lady, it's gone."

The girl lifted a tear-streaked face and scrutinized the now-dark niche. Seeing nothing there, she grasped Fabrizio's hand and raised herself up.

Unsure what to do, Fabrizio waited as Teresina composed herself. When she finally looked at him, it was as if for the first time. "Who are you?" she suddenly demanded.

"With permission, my lady," Fabrizio said, making a clumsy bow. "My name is Fabrizio. The magician's servant."

"Oh, yes. Did you see the ghost?" she asked.

"I did, my lady."

"What did you see?"

Fabrizio described the vision as best he could.

"There, I'm not insane."

"Not unless I am, too, my lady."

"No one else believes me."

"My lady," Fabrizio said, "your father, the king, does. That's why he called upon my master."

The princess shook her head. "My father is frightened but he didn't bid your master come. It was Count Scarazoni. I'm very grateful. When Mangus agrees there is a ghost, he'll be well rewarded. Not only will I insist my father pardon him, I'll make sure he's given a rich pension."

"Can you really do such things, my lady?" Fabrizio exclaimed, delighted by the prospect.

"I can. It's because of what happened to my brother, the prince," the girl confided solemnly.

"With permission, my lady, what about him?"

Teresina leaned forward. "He has vanished," she whispered into his ear.

"Vanished!"

"A few months ago he was sent as an emissary to the pope, in Rome," the girl explained. "He never reached the holy city. I believe he was murdered and the ghost we saw is . . . his."

Fabrizio felt queasy. "Does it look like him?"

"It's his face, his size and shape. So, you see, if something happened to my father, I would rule the kingdom."

Fabrizio considered the princess anew. If she could give Mangus his freedom *and* a pension, happiness would be reclaimed. Then and there, the boy vowed to make sure it happened.

"My lady," he said, "with permission, you need to know that my master is . . . shy about showing how clever he is."

"I heard him confess to being a magician at his trial," Teresina said. "I know the wonders he can do."

Fabrizio, inventing furiously, said, "My lady,

because my master wants to save his magic for special occasions, most times his sorcery is ... only pretend. I can assure you, though, the effects are just as fine. Sparkling candles. Colored smoke. Amazing words."

Teresina was puzzled. "I don't understand."

"It's just ... my master believes *reason* to be ... well, more powerful than magic."

Teresina looked at Fabrizio with alarm. "Are you saying your master does not believe in magic?"

"In ... his way."

"That's so silly!" the girl exclaimed. "Even Signore Addetto, who is a stupid man, has taught me that reasoning is a waste of time. Over and over again — he tells me I should simply do as I am told."

"My lady, I agree. Give me a lucky stone or a dead man's tooth over a hundred volumes of reason. But, for Mangus, magic ... *is* a kind of reason."

"Can you give me an example?"

"I should be pleased to," Fabrizio said. Plunging his hand into his pocket, he took out a tattered card. "Now, watch closely." With a few simple hand passes, he made the card disappear, only to pluck it from his own ear.

Teresina's eyes opened very wide. "But . . . that is magic!" she exclaimed.

"I would agree," Fabrizio said.

"If your master wishes to call such magic as that 'reason,' I don't care, not as long as he helps me. Fabrizio," she said, using his name for the first time, "why were you wandering?"

"My lady, I was clumsy enough to spill the water in our chamber. My master asked me to fetch more. When I tried to find the kitchens, I became lost."

"It's easy to get confused," the princess agreed. "The castello has fifty-two corridors connecting two hundred and thirty-three rooms. I've counted them myself.

"Beyond the open passages," she continued, "there are countless hidden ones. Very few know about them. It was my brother — the prince — who revealed them all to me. They can prove very useful.

"But, Fabrizio, I must ask, do you intend to tell your master that you and I saw the ghost?"

"Should I not?"

"Would he tell Count Scarazoni?"

"Forgive me, Teresina, my master is like no other man I know: He always tries to tell the truth. I've tried to argue him out of it. But I'm only a servant."

"Then you mustn't tell him what happened tonight or Scarazoni will learn of us. If the count discovered that we're friends, he'd become very angry. He guards me with great care. But, Fabrizio, promise you'll get Mangus to visit this place so he can see for himself the ghost is real."

"My lady, I don't know if I can."

"Fabrizio, didn't you save me from the ghost just now? Make it go away? Make a card vanish and then come back? Very well," Teresina continued before Fabrizio could reply, "then you'll make him come and believe. You do want him to be rewarded, don't you?"

"My lady, I go by the old saying 'A hungry chicken should never lay an empty egg.'"

"Good. Rule him as you are ruled by me, and he will have his reward."

"I promise," Fabrizio said in haste.

"Then we two are a conspiracy. Oh, Fabrizio," she cried, clapping her hands with glee, "I do so *love* conspiracies! Now, quickly, follow me, and I'll show you where your master sleeps." So saying, she hurried down the corridor. Fabrizio scrambled after her.

Halting before a large tapestry that hung against the wall, Teresina lifted one corner and revealed a small door recessed in the wall. She opened it and passed through. Amazed, Fabrizio followed.

The tiny chamber they entered was illuminated by moonlight, which seeped in from a high, narrow window. Other than cobwebs that stretched from wall to wall, the chamber contained nothing more than a flight of stairs that spiraled into darkness.

"Where are we?" Fabrizio asked, feeling compelled to keep his voice low.

"It's one of the secret passages I spoke of," Teresina said with a giggle.

Round and round they went until Fabrizio became quite dizzy. At the top they came to yet another door. Teresina paused. "Go through that door," she said. "Your chamber will be just around the left corner. A soldier will be there. You can't miss it."

Just as Fabrizio made a move to leave, she held him back. "Fabrizio," she said, "whenever you see me — in the company of others — act as others would expect. I am exalted and noble. You are low and common. It would be unwise for us to be observed speaking to one another.

You can't imagine how closely I'm watched. Most times I'm no better off than a prisoner.

"But we shall see each other again tomorrow at midnight," she said. "That will be after you get Mangus to look at the niche." So saying, she opened the door and all but pushed Fabrizio into a hallway. The door closed behind him. When he turned back to look, both princess and door seemed to have vanished.

But even as he stared at the place, the door popped open. Teresina poked her head out. "Fabrizio," she called, "remember your promises. Don't tell Mangus what happened tonight. But for him to earn a great reward, you must convince him to see the ghost. And always — beware of Count Scarazoni!" So saying, she shut the door, leaving Fabrizio alone.

For a moment Fabrizio stared at the door. Then, taking a deep breath, he turned the corner and went down the hall. Within moments he came upon the guard who had been posted by their door. He was still asleep.

Within the chamber the candle was all but out. Mangus lay asleep. Fabrizio, relieved he would not need to explain his long absence, took a place on the floor by the door.

But he could not sleep. His mind kept going

over all that had occurred. The ghost. The princess's words that it was Count Scarazoni who had requested Mangus to come to the castello. His own observation of the ghost, and his promise to the princess that he would not tell Mangus what he had seen, along with his second promise to get his master to view the niche.

Then there was news that the king's son had disappeared, perhaps been *murdered*.

But, as far as Fabrizio was concerned, the most important thing was Princess Teresina's vow to do well by Mangus. Here was an extraordinary opportunity. He must make the most of it.

Pleased with the prospect, Fabrizio closed his eyes and was asleep within seconds.

So soundly did the boy sleep, he failed to hear the steps that crept away from outside the door. Someone had been listening to see if he had spoken to Mangus.

chapter 8

In the morning it was only when he heard Mangus moving about that Fabrizio woke. After the two had completed their prayers, Mangus announced he had something in particular to say. Certain he was about to be asked about his whereabouts during the night, Fabrizio tried to think how he would answer.

"Fabrizio," Mangus began, his tone firm, "last night, when we arrived in the castello, though you promised you wouldn't, you performed a bit of so-called magic."

Relieved, Fabrizio hung his head, even as he remembered the magic items he'd stashed away in his pocket. "Master," he replied, "they were being disrespectful toward you."

Mangus sighed. "Fabrizio, if you buy with ignorance, you will be paid with the same coin."

"But, Master, you know what people say, 'False gold often buys more than iron.'"

"Fabrizio, a fool is paid in folly."

"Master," the boy retorted, "if a foolish man makes a map, let him journey alone."

"Ah," Mangus replied, "but until all men are wise, the wise must act for all men."

"Master," Fabrizio said, "just because a flea needs blood to live, am I obliged to carry him on *my* skin?"

Mangus smiled. "Fabrizio, enough of this banter. Last night, did you bring water?"

"Master . . . I could not find the kitchens."

"You should be able to find them now. Go. We need some food. But, please, no more tricks!"

"Your commands are silver, Master."

"Fabrizio!"

"Yes, Master."

"Respect is golden."

Though many more lamps and candles were burning, Fabrizio found the castello corridors as dim and clammy as they had been the night before. The humidity and heat were so great, it was as if the building itself were sweating. But, unlike the night, when the halls were deserted, so many people were going about their business that Fabrizio felt as if he were back in the city.

Soldiers were everywhere. Some were patrolling, while others were standing guard with dogs, intently watching all who passed. Fabrizio wondered if they were looking for spies.

At first he thought he went unnoticed. But gradually he became aware that soldiers were noticing him as he went by, nudging one another, sometimes even backing away. It made Fabrizio unwilling to ask for directions.

Only when a woman with a load of wash upon her head came by did he ask the way to the kitchens. At first the woman smiled, but her mood changed quickly. "Aren't you the magician's boy?" she asked, her voice hushed.

Fabrizio hardly knew what to answer. Their visit was supposed to be a secret. Then he remembered that his master had been recognized by the soldiers. And there had been his trick. With a sinking heart, he wondered how many in the castello knew of their presence.

The woman backed away. "If it's the kitchens you want, you'll find them at the lower level," she said. Then she turned on her heel and all but ran away.

Following the woman's directions, Fabrizio

soon reached the kitchens. They consisted of seven large, cavelike, barrel-vaulted rooms connected one to the other in a long row. Food was everywhere: hanging from ceilings; on tables; on the floor in sacks and barrels. The air was full of delicious smells, too. Herbs and spices, garlic and onions, all fused with the splendid fragrance of fish, meats, cakes, and savories. Meanwhile, a crowd of cooks and bakers, along with many helpers, were standing about open fires and at the long tables, mixing, cutting, stirring, pounding, and shaping.

Most of the cooks' helpers were boys and girls. A motley crew, they ran about and shouted as they worked. No one paid Fabrizio any notice.

Looking about, he spied a boy who appeared to be a little beyond his own age. A tall, lanky, long-nosed fellow, he had scruffy hair that fell, masklike, over his eyes. The hair did not seem to interfere with his work — which was slicing turnips with an extremely sharp knife. His agility was considerable.

Fabrizio drew close. "Good morning, friend," he said. "Can you tell me how I might get some food for my master's breakfast table?"

The boy paused in his work and glanced up. His face was dirty, but his eyes were bright. "I'm sorry," he said gruffly, "we're not allowed to talk to strangers." He returned to his turnips.

Miffed, Fabrizio turned to a woman in a corner sitting midst a cloud of feathers that came from a plump goose she was plucking. Though Fabrizio stood before her patiently, it was as if he were not there. She kept her eyes on her goose.

At last Fabrizio said, "Good woman, can you tell me where I may find some breakfast?"

The woman, refusing to lift her eyes, snapped, "Be off! I can't talk to you."

Determined not to be thwarted again, Fabrizio looked around. That time he spied a large, fat man with a florid, red face and massive arms, sitting on a high stool. He had a white cap on his head, and a large key affixed to a chain that went round his tublike stomach. It was the master cook.

Fabrizio approached. "With permission, Signore," he began, "I'm in need of some food for my master."

The cook drew himself up haughtily. "Do you dare speak to me?" he snapped. "Throw this beggar out of here!"

All work stopped. The kitchen became still.

Deciding he had to do something to assert himself, Fabrizio plunged his right hand into his pocket even as he held his left hand high over his head. "Behold!" he cried, showing his left hand to be bare and open. All eyes went to this hand. Fabrizio made a fist. Next he shoved his right thumb into that fist and removed it, showing the right hand to be open and bare. Finally, he reached back into his left fist with fingers of his right hand and pulled out a long green ribbon.

As gasps of astonishment came from the crowd, Fabrizio flipped the ribbon onto the master cook's lap.

The cook stared with terror-filled eyes at the ribbon that lay upon his belly. "Why . . . why . . . that's magic!" he cried. Leaping off his stool, he brushed away the ribbon as if it were a poisonous snake.

"That's what people call it," Fabrizio replied coolly, even as he slipped the skin-colored thumb-glove he'd worn back into his pocket. The glove had concealed the ribbon. No one had noticed his simple manipulation.

The master cook hurriedly doffed his cap and made a clumsy bow. "Signore, you . . . honor us by . . . your presence," he stammered. "Was it . . . food you desire?"

"Breakfast for my master," Fabrizio replied.

"Who . . . is your master?"

"Mangus the Magician."

There was a murmur from those in the kitchen. The master cook, his face pale, held up his hands in appeal. "Signore, please, take as much as you want. And with profound regrets that you even had to ask. It's an honor serving you."

Bowing and scraping, he clapped his hands. "A bowl," he cried. "Instantly! Rinaldo!"

The kitchen boy who had ignored Fabrizio moments before rushed forward with a large wooden bowl.

"Fill it!" the cook commanded, and clapped his hands again. Other kitchen workers hurriedly filled the bowl with bread, meats, and fish as well as confections of all kinds. It was enough to feed five.

"Will this suffice?" he asked Fabrizio as he continued to bow.

"For the moment," Fabrizio allowed.

"If you will follow," the master cook said, "the boy will take the food to your chamber. And, Signore," he added, "in the future, you need only send one of your servants."

"I am the magician's only trusted servant," Fabrizio said grandly.

Under the awestruck eyes of the staff, Fabrizio swept out of the kitchen behind the boy who bore the bowl. As he passed out of the rooms, he heard the master cook cry out, "Do not cross that boy! Give him whatever he wants. If you don't, he'll put a spell on you!"

A grinning Fabrizio marched away.

chapter 9

As Fabrizio and the kitchen boy headed back to Mangus's chamber, the boy — who was leading the way — kept glancing back around. Fabrizio, deciding the boy was in awe of him, squared his shoulder and began to swagger.

Upon reaching a narrow passage, the boy suddenly stopped. "Please . . . Signore," he stammered, his head bowed so Fabrizio could not see his face, "you must forgive me. I wasn't trying to ignore you when you spoke to me in the kitchen. We're not permitted to talk with strangers."

"You needn't have worried," Fabrizio assured him haughtily.

"You see," the kitchen boy went on, "the last time I did so — it was to another newly arrived servant — I was all but thrown out of the castello. I can't let that happen."

"Why are they so severe?" Fabrizio asked.

"Spies," the boy replied. "They say they are everywhere.

"Who says?" Fabrizio asked. "Your master cook?"

"Oh, no, Signore, the cook only enforces the rules. It's Count Scarazoni who holds sway in the castello. But, Signore," the boy continued, "though I'm the lowest in the kitchen, I heard about the wondrous feat of magic you performed for the soldiers upon your arrival. You made a purse of gold vanish."

"It was only a coin," Fabrizio protested mildly.

"Whatever it was, it's all the talk this morning. It's made people very anxious."

"Anxious?"

"Because you are a boy of great power."

Fabrizio drew himself up. "My master and I are here only to serve the king," he said.

The kitchen boy looked up. "Ah, but Signore," he asked, "will that service be for good or evil?"

Taken aback by the question, Fabrizio studied the kitchen boy, trying to read his eyes. But the boy hastily turned away, as though fearful Fabrizio might discover something.

"Tell me your name once again," Fabrizio demanded.

"Rinaldo, Signore."

"Where are you from, Rinaldo?"

"Pergamontio, Signore. Where else?"

Fabrizio stared at the boy, wondering if *he* could be a spy? All he said, however, was, "My master is waiting, Rinaldo."

"Forgive me, Signore," the boy said, making a low bow. "I should not be wasting your time."

The two started off, Rinaldo in the lead again. Suddenly, he cried, "Signore! Here, quickly!" Even as he spoke, he pushed against a framed portrait set against the wall. To Fabrizio's amazement, the painting swung in like a door. "Hurry!" Rinaldo said.

Without thinking, Fabrizio followed, finding himself in a narrow enclosure. Rinaldo pulled the door shut, plunging the tiny area into total darkness.

"Where are we?" Fabrizio demanded, keeping his voice low. "Why did you lead me in here?"

"Didn't you see?" Rinaldo whispered. "Down the hallway. Count Scarazoni was in the corridor talking to someone."

"What of it?"

"It's as I told you," Rinaldo explained. "No

one in the kitchen may talk to strangers. If Scarazoni saw, it could go badly for me."

Fabrizio frowned. "Why should he care if you and I speak?"

Momentarily, Rinaldo was hesitant. Then, as if making up his mind, he said, "Signore, follow me." The next moment, he pushed open another door.

This second door opened into a long, narrow room that was suffused with the smell of incense. One wall was paneled with fine wood and had framed paintings of saints and martyrs. Opposite the entryway were stained-glass windows through which streamed multicolored lines of sunlight. On the inside walls were windows of cloudy, green glass.

At the head of the room stood an altar upon which was a golden cross made bright by a steadily burning altar candle. Nearby was an enormous candelabra with a large, round, polished silver plate affixed behind the candle, designed to reflect light.

Facing the altar were four chairs and prayer stools. A long, coffinlike box — for vestments, Fabrizio supposed — stood near the large candelabra. One end bore candle drippings. The front of the room — behind the altar — was completely dark.

"Where are we?" Fabrizio demanded, his voice hushed as he crossed himself.

"The king's family's private chapel."

"How did you know of that entry?"

"It's a servants' passage, Signore. For bringing food."

"Is it safe to be here?"

"You need not worry. No one is likely to come."

Fabrizio, unable to think of a worse place to be, groaned inwardly. "Why did you bring me here?"

"I've decided to ask you something."

"What?"

Instead of answering, Rinaldo set the food bowl down and paced about, as if trying to settle his mind. At last he said, "Signore, can you foretell the future?"

Fabrizio, recalling the tarot cards with uneasiness, said, "There were times I've done so. Why do you ask?"

"I wish I knew the fate of Pergamontio, Signore."

"Is that why you brought me here?" Fabrizio

said with scorn. "To waste my time thinking about such things? It's for our betters to decide the kingdom's fate."

Rinaldo drew close. "But, Signore, at the moment there is only death in our future."

"Death!" Fabrizio cried.

Rinaldo brushed the hair out of his eyes. "There is an evil power in this castello," he said with care.

Immediately thinking of the ghost, Fabrizio wondered how Rinaldo knew about it. "What are you talking about?" he asked.

Instead of replying, Rinaldo turned away and resumed his pacing about the chapel.

"Signore," Rinaldo said at last, "there are many here — people like you and me — who want nothing more than to attach themselves to the one who will rid us of this evil."

"What are you talking about?" Fabrizio demanded.

"I just saw your magic, Signore," the kitchen boy went on. "I had already heard about it. Many have. What the people of Pergamontio need is a leader. A leader such as you."

"Me?" Fabrizio cried, taken aback.

"Signore, your magic can help us achieve the downfall of Count Scarazoni."

Fabrizio was speechless. Rinaldo was talking treason.

The kitchen boy drew close. "Signore, rumor has it that the young prince may never return from his mission. If he is gone, Princess Teresina is next in line. If something should happen to her . . . do you know who would become king?"

Fabrizio shook his head.

"Count Scarazoni."

"Scarazoni!"

"It's true. Because he . . ." He stopped talking.

"What's the matter?"

"The door! Quickly! I mustn't be seen! Hide!" Shoving Fabrizio aside, Rinaldo snatched up the food bowl and plunged back into the cabinet, shutting the door behind him. Fabrizio tried to follow by pulling the door open. It would not move. Hardly knowing where to turn, he rushed behind the altar and knelt, praying the darkness would protect him. Even as he did, the front door of the chapel opened, bringing a shaft of light into the room. Someone was entering the chapel.

chapter 10

Though fearful of being seen, Fabrizio's curiosity made him rise slightly. Squinting into the gloom, he saw Count Scarazoni entering the chapel. With his long, lean face and pointed beard, he looked like the Devil himself. Fabrizio was so frightened, he made the sign of the cross over his heart.

For a moment, Scarazoni stood before the chapel door, looking in. Then he made a half turn. "It's empty," he said to someone while he himself moved farther into the chapel. "We can talk here."

"It's very dark," came a second voice. A man's voice.

"I can give you only a short time," Scarazoni said.

Teresina's tutor, Signore Addetto, entered.

More alarmed than ever, Fabrizio ducked down and contented himself with listening.

"Now, Signore," Count Scarazoni began, "I am prepared to hear you out."

"I'm very troubled, my lord," the tutor said.

Scarazoni snorted. "Signore," he said, "may I remind you that it was you who suggested this plan of action to me."

"Indeed, my lord. It sits heavy upon me. But this ghost, my lord, was not part of the plan."

"Mangus will deal with it."

"My lord," Addetto replied, "I distinctly heard him say he does not believe in spirits."

"He doesn't," Scarazoni said. "Which is why he will take pains to dismiss the girl's illusions. And if he doesn't, his life is forfeit."

"But, my lord, the man is a sorcerer. I . . . I fear him."

"You are fearful of too many things, Signore," Scarazoni returned. "All of Mangus's so-called magic is a sham. There's absolutely nothing to be alarmed about."

"So you say, my lord," Addetto said meekly. "But you are powerful, and I —"

"He's here to serve my purpose," Scarazoni said, cutting the man off.

"But, what," Addetto whined, "if Mangus discovers my role and informs the king? My life will be over."

"Mangus has no interest in you. And the king believes in his magic. When Mangus tells him there is no ghost, the marriage will take place — as planned — in three days' time. That's why I brought him here."

"Count Scarazoni," Addetto said timidly, "you don't believe in ghosts, do you?"

"Not at all."

"Forgive me, my lord, I do. I think this thing has come back to reveal the part I have played."

"Why should this so-called ghost care about you?"

"Because it was my idea. . . ."

"Do you doubt the princess has invented the ghost so as to avoid her marriage?"

"My lord. I . . . don't know."

"Didn't I make the king and queen agree to the marriage?"

"You did, my lord. You certainly did."

"The fools! They don't grasp how much it will weaken them. I shall marry the princess, then take the king's throne when I choose to do so. Your task is to keep instructing the girl to do what her betters tell her to do."

"I will, my lord, I assure you I will."

"You have my protection," Scarazoni said sharply. "What more can you want?"

"My lord, I fear for my soul. I have conspired against the king. Blood may be on my hands. My lord, has . . . has there been any . . . news of the prince?"

"None."

"Not a trace?"

"I have people looking everywhere."

"My lord, I . . . I truly think it's his ghost who has come."

"The prince was killed," Scarazoni said. "There is no more to say. Now, do not interfere with the plan. No more talk."

"Yes, my lord. Of course . . ."

Fabrizio could hear the two men walk out of the chapel, and the door shut behind them.

Astounded at all he had heard, Fabrizio searched frantically for the secret door, found it, and pushed against it. This time, it opened. That led him into the boxlike cabinet. Once there, he opened the other door and found himself back in the corridor. The framed portrait swung back in place. Moreover, Rinaldo was waiting, food bowl still in his hands.

"Where did you go?" Fabrizio demanded.

"Why did you leave me that way? That was treason you were talking!"

The kitchen boy smiled. "Signore, I'm merely a kitchen boy who —" Abruptly, he cut himself off. A look of alarm had come into his eyes.

Fabrizio, turning to see what had frightened the boy, saw Count Scarazoni coming in their direction. This time, there was no place to hide.

Hoping Scarazoni would want nothing of him, Fabrizio pressed himself against the wall and bowed his head. But, instead of passing, Count Scarazoni stopped. "Boy," he snapped.

Fabrizio looked up. "Yes, my lord."

"I was on my way to your master," Scarazoni said. "Take a message to him and save me steps."

"Yes, my lord," Fabrizio murmured.

"You there," he barked to Rinaldo, who was close by, head bowed. "What are you doing here?"

"Food for a guest," the boy mumbled, keeping his face averted.

"Step farther back!" Scarazoni ordered.

Rinaldo moved away quickly.

"Now then," Scarazoni said, speaking in hushed tones to Fabrizio. "The king wishes Mangus to meet with the princess this morning so that he may question her. Return immediately and inform him so."

"My lord, with permission, may he break-fast?"

Scarazoni peered around to make sure Rinaldo had not drawn closer. Satisfied, he drew closer; so close, his beard tickled Fabrizio's ear. "Let him eat his fill. But tell your master this: As far as I am concerned, the girl is hysterical. She has invented the ghost. Inform your master that if he can convince the king of this, I will give him back his liberties and provide a rich pension."

"Yes . . . my lord," Fabrizio stammered.

"But," Scarazoni continued, "if he does not free the princess of her delusions, he shall suffer for it."

"Yes, my lord."

"Repeat to him what I have said," Count Scarazoni concluded. "I will send a soldier for him shortly." With that, he strode away, leaving an astonished Fabrizio to watch him go.

Recalling that Rinaldo was waiting, he turned about. The kitchen boy had kept back, head bent over, staring at his food bowl. But then he looked up. "What did Scarazoni say to you?" he demanded.

"It was a message for my master," Fabrizio returned. "Not for you."

Rinaldo frowned. "And when he came into the chapel, was he alone?"

"He was with the princess's tutor."

"Was he?" Rinaldo cried. "The dog!"

"What's that to you?"

Instead of answering, the kitchen boy turned and moved along the corridor.

As they went along, Fabrizio wished he had not spoken to Rinaldo at all. Instead, he put his mind to informing Mangus about the count's message. But recalling his promise to do no tricks, he decided not to tell his master about his experience in the kitchen or his conversation with the boy.

chapter 11

When Fabrizio returned to the cell, Mangus bid Rinaldo to set the food bowl down, then dismissed him. As the kitchen boy left, he turned to Fabrizio and said, "Signore, call upon me if you need any more assistance." Making a bow, he left.

"Fabrizio," Mangus said when Rinaldo had gone, "did that boy call you *'Signore?'*"

Fabrizio hung his head. "I think so, Master."

"What have you done now?"

Fabrizio shrugged. "You know how it is, Master: The lowly worm thinks anything above him can fly." Then, wanting to divert Mangus, he said, "I have a message from Count Scarazoni," and he repeated what had been said to him.

Mangus was surprised. "Are you sure he said exactly those words, that he does *not* believe the princess has seen a ghost?"

"I'm certain, Master. And he says he will reward you well if you prove it. But, Master, you'll be proud of me. I have much more to tell you."

"Do you? Good. We shall eat and talk. I, for one, am famished."

As Fabrizio laid out the food before Mangus, he said, "Master, by pure accident, I found myself in the king's chapel. No sooner was I there than Count Scarazoni came in. Naturally, I hid. But I heard him talk."

"Fabrizio," Mangus cried with alarm, "you'll get yourself thrown into a dungeon. It's wrong to spy."

"Forgive me, Master. Would you rather I didn't tell you what I heard?"

"One often finds life under dead stones," Mangus said with a sigh.

As Fabrizio stuffed himself with food, he told Mangus what Count Scarazoni and the tutor Addetto had said; to wit:

That the princess was about to be married to Count Scarazoni;

That this marriage, moreover, was a scheme

made up by Signore Addetto so that Scarazoni could become the king;

That Count Scarazoni believed the princess had invented the ghost to get out of the marriage;

That it was Count Scarazoni who had wanted Mangus to come to the castello so as to prove that there was no ghost;

That if Mangus did so, the count would restore his liberties and provide a pension.

"Fabrizio," Mangus said when he heard it all, "if what you say is true, this matter is far more dangerous than I had thought. But why should Scarazoni want this marriage so much? It's the king's son who shall inherit the title."

"Ah, Master, I'm like a nail without a head! How could I forget? The prince has vanished!"

"Vanished?"

"Master," Fabrizio whispered, "Scarazoni said the prince was killed."

"It's shocking," Mangus said. "To whom was the count speaking?"

Once again, Fabrizio leaned forward and whispered, "The princess's tutor, Signore Addetto. And, Master, the whole plan was *his* idea."

"That man's a fool," Mangus said scornfully.

"And in a game far too dangerous for him." He lapsed into thought.

After a while, Fabrizio said, "Will you question the princess, Master?"

"To be sure."

Fabrizio, suddenly remembering his promise to the princess that he would urge Mangus to visit the niche, said, "Master, if you prove there is no ghost, I think you will be helping Scarazoni in his plot to overthrow the king."

"That may be true."

"But . . . do you wish to do that?"

"Fabrizio," Mangus said with care, "my life's work is to search for truth with reason. Quite often, reason leads us to places neither expected nor wanted. I promised the king I would seek the truth. Can I turn from reason just because it does not please me? No. On the other hand, Fabrizio, if she truly believes there is a ghost, if she is truly mad —"

"*Mad?*" Fabrizio exclaimed.

"What else can you call someone who sees something that is not there?"

Fabrizio felt like shouting, *But I saw it!* Instead, he said, "Master, last week I spoke to a boy I know. He insists the world is round because his patron told him so. Stupid, yes, for any donkey can see with their own eyes that the world is flat. But is the boy mad to believe what his patron told him? Would you call every person who believes an impossible thing 'mad'?"

"Fabrizio, if one sees what isn't there to see, madness is the only possible explanation. So, yes, if your friend insists the world is round, alas, he is mad."

Fabrizio sighed.

Mangus stood up, brushed crumbs from his beard and garments, rubbed his hands, then gazed at the boy for a moment as if to measure him. "Fabrizio, I'm glad you're here with me."

The boy glowed with pride.

"You are good to remind me that the ways of reason and truth are never easy. When I question the princess, I want you to keep your eyes on Scarazoni."

"Yes, Master, I will. But can you make any sense of all this?"

"Whether or not this marriage is wise is not for me to say. But I'm beginning to think Count Scarazoni is correct. The princess has made up this ghost to avoid marriage. Now, come along, we should be going."

A soldier was at the door. But no sooner did they start down the hall than they saw Signore

Addetto rushing toward them. "Signore!" the tutor called to Mangus. He kept bowing and squeezing his hands together. His face was in a sweat.

Mangus paused.

"With permission, Signore," Addetto whispered, his eyes full of fear. "A word with you! Please! It's urgent."

"Hurry on," the soldier called. "We're keeping Count Scarazoni waiting."

"I'm on my way to see the princess," Mangus said to the tutor. "When I return to my chamber, we can talk."

As they continued on, Fabrizio looked back. The tutor was staring after them, white-faced.

chapter 12

Count Scarazoni led Mangus and Fabrizio into a narrow, unadorned room to meet with Princess Teresina. She was sitting rigidly on a chair.

Mangus, in consideration of his age, was allowed to sit. Fabrizio stood behind him.

"My lady," Mangus began, speaking slowly and kindly, "your father, the king, has brought me here to help you in your time of trouble. I have been given permission to question you regarding this *thing* you have observed. Do not think I'm being disrespectful. I wish to be helpful."

"I understand," Teresina said in a flat voice.

Mangus: "Yesterday you said you saw this

vision four times in a place not far from your quarters. Just where was this spot?"

Princess Teresina: "Near my chambers, in a niche."

Mangus: "With permission, describe again what you saw."

Princess Teresina: "It was more light than body."

Mangus: "No corporeal substance, such as you or I have?"

Princess Teresina: "None."

Mangus: "Can you then describe its face?"

Princess Teresina: "Only that it had a face."

Mangus: "No more?"

Princess Teresina: "Arms, for it beckoned me toward it."

Mangus: "You said it spoke to you."

Teresina: "Not with words."

Mangus: "If not with words, Princess, how then?"

Princess Teresina: "Its manner."

Mangus: "What did it say to you?"

Princess Teresina: "It wished revenge."

Mangus: "Revenge for what?"

Princess Teresina: "Its death."

Mangus: "With no words spoken, how can you be so sure?"

When Princess Teresina hesitated, Fabrizio leaned forward to hear her answer.

Finally, the girl said, "I know it."

Mangus: "Do you think you know whose ghost this is?"

Princess Teresina: "My brother's."

"Brother!" Scarazoni cried with such vehemence, Fabrizio started. "You never said so before, Princess."

Teresina said nothing but continued to stare ahead.

Mangus studied his hands, then said softly, "My lady, I did not know your brother — the prince — had died."

Princess Teresina: "If I have seen his ghost, he must be dead."

"Princess," Scarazoni interjected again, "your brother is in Rome. Cease talking nonsense. Mangus, change the subject."

As Mangus rubbed his hands, Fabrizio pondered what the princess had said about the ghost. It fit with all his own observations the night before. Then he remembered he was supposed to be watching Count Scarazoni. He shifted slightly.

Scarazoni's face was red. His brow knit. He had become very angry.

Mangus resumed his questioning. "My lady, do you think this vision meant you harm?"

Princess Teresina: "No."

Mangus: "Why?"

Princess Teresina: "My brother would not hurt me."

Mangus: "My lady, with due respect, the king, your father, the queen, your mother, as well as Count Scarazoni, when they went to observe this thing at the same place, they saw nothing. How do you explain this?"

Princess Teresina: "I cannot."

Mangus: "Do you believe you alone are privileged to see what you saw?"

Princess Teresina: "My lady-in-waiting saw it."

Mangus: "Alas, she is gone. Might any other person observe this thing?"

Fabrizio thought she darted a quick look at him.

Mangus, sensing her hesitation, again asked, "Princess, *do* you think someone else might see this thing?"

Princess Teresina: "Yes."

Mangus: "Do you believe *I* could see it?"

Princess Teresina: "Yes."

Mangus rubbed his hands for warmth. "Princess," he asked in his most gentle tone, "with permission, there is a rumor that you are to be married. Is this true?"

"Who told you that?" Scarazoni interrupted. His face had turned pale.

Mangus turned to him. "My lord," he said, speaking very carefully, "it is only what one hears. Do you wish me to withdraw this question, too?"

The princess shifted her eyes to Scarazoni.

"You may answer it," Scarazoni said.

Princess Teresina: "Yes, I am to be married."

Mangus: "Are you pleased about this?"

Princess Teresina: "As my tutor, Signore Addetto, has taught me, my joy is in doing what my father and mother ask me to do. My happiness is what is good for Pergamontio."

Mangus: "When is this marriage to take place?"

Princess Teresina: "In two days."

Mangus: "That seems very soon."

Princess Teresina: "My father has consulted the stars. It's the most favorable time. Otherwise we must wait at least two years."

Mangus nodded and then stood. "Very well, my lady. I have no further questions." He bowed.

Turning to Scarazoni, he said, "My lord, I should like to see the place where the *thing* was observed. Is that possible?"

It took a moment for the count to respond to the question. Fabrizio could see that he was still upset. Then the count said, "If you wish."

While Princess Teresina was guided back to her room, by a soldier, Mangus, Scarazoni, and Fabrizio went to the place where the ghost had been observed. As they went along, Fabrizio glanced at his master. The old man seemed to be full of energy, more than Fabrizio had seen for a long time. It was, he mused, as if this need to deal with the dead had brought him new life.

"Count Scarazoni," Mangus said, "I received your message. You said you did not believe this ghost was real."

"The princess is trying to avoid her duty," the count said curtly.

"Her duty?"

"The marriage."

"Yet it is common for nobility to be married when young," Mangus said smoothly. "May I ask whom she is to marry?"

"Me."

"I congratulate you."

Scarazoni suddenly stopped. "Mangus," he demanded, "how did you learn of this marriage?"

Mangus made a casual nod toward Fabrizio. "My boy is like a sponge that soaks up rumors.

He heard it from some common sort and passed it on to me."

Count Scarazoni glowered at Fabrizio. To Mangus he said, "The marriage must not be talked about."

"But is it true," Mangus persisted, "what she said, that the king has chosen the date because of his study of the stars?"

"No more!" Scarazoni snapped. But then he added, "The prince has gone on a diplomatic mission. He is merely overdue. You may ignore what the princess said about that. Indeed, you must not — on pain of death — speak of these matters to anyone. Your task is to deal with the ghost and only the ghost." He started to walk away.

"My lord," Mangus called after him, "Signore Addetto, the tutor, wishes to talk to me."

Scarazoni looked around angrily. "Does he?"

"May I speak to him?"

"No. You may not. The man's a fool. Here is the spot," the count informed Mangus.

They were in a long, wide corridor — some eight feet in width — faced by stone on floor and wall. The corridor was *two* levels high: the level upon which they were walking, and another some twelve feet above, where a series of windows ranged.

It was the same place, Fabrizio noted, that he had been the night before. But in the greater light Fabrizio could see that the niche was rectangular in shape, narrow and shallow, built into the stone wall some three feet off the floor. It looked — he thought uneasily — like a coffin.

"My lord," Mangus asked, "can you think of any reason why this vision should have been seen *here* rather than in another place?"

Count Scarazoni shrugged. "It is close to the princess's quarters."

Mangus stared at the spot silently. "My lord," he said softly, "how is it that this niche is empty?"

Scarazoni considered for a moment. It seemed to Fabrizio he was deciding whether or not to reply. "I have no idea," he answered.

"Might there," Mangus continued, "have once been a statue here? Some saint, perchance, some figure of Our Blessed Savior?"

"What difference does that make?" Scarazoni said with annoyance.

"Perhaps none," Mangus acknowledge. "But, sometimes, my lord, as it is said, a good answer may lead to a better question. If there was a figure here, it would be useful to know when it was removed and . . . by whom."

Count Scarazoni gazed at the niche. "You are right. I shall make inquiries."

Mangus turned to study the corridor. "Would all these lamps be lit at night?"

Fabrizio almost said out loud, *No*, but did not dare.

"At the time," Scarazoni said, "that the princess saw the ghost, most would have burned low or have been out."

Fabrizio could have acknowledged the truth of that.

"As I understand it," Mangus said, "the princess has her rooms there." He pointed down the corridor. Then he shifted to indicate the other direction. "Whose chambers are nearest in that direction?"

"Her brother, the prince."

"And beyond that?"

"The king and queen."

Mangus looked up. "Those windows, there," he said, pointing to the second — higher — row of windows. "Into what do they look?"

"Rooms for other members of the court. And the family chapel."

"No doubt," Mangus continued, "there is another level below us, is that correct?"

Scarazoni nodded.

"Who resides there?"

"Still more persons of the court."

"And your quarters?" Mangus inquired gently. Fabrizio was certain this was the question his master was leading to.

"Beyond the king's," Scarazoni said, pointing along the hall from where they stood.

Mangus returned to examining the niche in great detail, feeling about the area with his hand. Suddenly he plucked out something and held it close to his eyes.

"Have you found something, Master?" Fabrizio asked.

"It is a bit of wood," he said, holding it out. "Some blue paint remains, the kind of blue as might adorn the Holy Virgin. My lord, may I suggest that there *was* a statue here. With permission, I should like to know when it was removed."

Count Scarazoni nodded grimly.

"My lord, might I request that my boy climb into this place?"

"Yes."

An uncomfortable Fabrizio attempted to squeeze himself into the niche. It was impossible. No human could. It was further proof — as if Fabrizio needed more — that what he had seen the night before was no living thing.

chapter 13

F abrizio," Mangus said when the two of them returned to the privacy of their chamber, "I trust you no longer believe there is a ghost."

"Why do you say that, Master?"

"Reason, Fabrizio," he replied, *"reason.* When I questioned Princess Teresina, even you must have noticed how unable she was to say what this so-called ghost had said, or even was. As for her belief that it's her brother's spirit, no one else makes the claim the prince was murdered. Not even his father, the king. Beyond all else, Fabrizio, she is the sole person who has seen the so-called ghost."

"Her lady-in-waiting saw it," Fabrizio pointed out.

"So the princess claims. But this lady took the veil and has vowed not to speak. If just one other person could tell me that he saw this *thing*," Mangus said, "it might change my reasoning, but no one has."

Fabrizio stared at his boots.

"Now then, Mangus said, "how did Scarazoni react to the interview?"

"He grew very upset."

"At any particular points?"

"It was when you spoke of the marriage and of the king's son."

"Ah!"

"Master, with permission, I have an idea."

"Speak."

Fabrizio edged closer to Mangus. "I think," he whispered, "the count murdered the king's son, and it's the prince's ghost who has come back seeking justice. The whole world knows ghosts act just that way."

Mangus shook his head. "Just now, when I examined the spot where the princess believed she saw the ghost, I found some evidence that — I'm sure — will prove a statue had been recently removed." He held out the sliver of wood he had picked up. "Why else would this remain?"

Fabrizio examined the sliver. It had a blue

tint and was about two and a half times longer than his thumb but only half as wide. "What does it have to do with the ghost?" he asked.

Mangus smiled. "I suspect the statue was removed so that the princess would see something there. A niche would make for a most ghostly appearance. In other words, we need to discover who removed the statue, when, and why."

"What do you think?"

"Fabrizio, if the cart is the conclusion, and oxen are the facts, is it better for the beasts to pull or push the cart?"

"To pull, master."

"Exactly. So let us have the facts first."

"Master, you asked Scarazoni to find out."

"I'd rather search for myself. But I do believe the count is right. This entire affair is connected to the princess's forthcoming marriage.

"Yes," Mangus mused out loud, "Signore Addetto concocts this idea of marriage to Scarazoni. The count acts to bring it about. Though the marriage frightens her — how old is she? Eight, nine . . . ?"

"Ten, I think."

"The girl does what she is told to do. Her father, the king, wildly superstitious, consults the stars to pick a marriage date.

"Suddenly, Princess Teresina sees a ghost, just the thing that would make the king hold off the marriage.

"Scarazoni, aware that I don't believe in ghosts but knowing that the king thinks me a magician, brings us here because only I can convince the king the ghost is fiction. If I do so, the marriage will take place. There, I've solved it all."

"But, Master," Fabrizio pleaded, "if you visited that place at night, perhaps you would see something for yourself."

"I assure you, I would see nothing."

Fabrizio looked thoughtfully at Mangus. "Master, did you not just say your esteemed reasoning requires you to see for yourself — to have the facts — and *then* decide?"

Mangus scowled. "It would be a waste of time. Instead, I want you to roam the castello. Find out about the missing statue."

"What will it tell you?"

"I suspect that if we find who removed the statue and when it was done, we shall know more about the princess and her so-called ghost."

"Why don't you just ask her about it?"

Mangus smiled. "The fastest way to judge the

honesty of a person, Fabrizio, is to ask a question for which you already have the answer."

"But, Master, with permission, does not that make the questioner a liar?"

"Fabrizio, must you always turn the things I say around?"

"Forgive me, Master, but you know the old saying 'There are two ways to look through a window.'"

"You wear me out with your wise sayings. Here, take the bit of wood and search. I'll remain here."

"Yes, Master, I'll go at once."

Mangus lay back on his bed. "Fabrizio, I worry about my good wife," he said. "She must be in great distress about us."

"Signora Sophia has great faith, Master."

"She will need it."

By the time Fabrizio left their chamber, he had already made up his mind: Despite what Mangus had said, he was going to ask the princess about the statue. As for his failure to get Mangus to view the niche, he was not sure what he would say about that.

Happily, he had already gained a sense of how the castello lay, and he was able to reach the area near the princess's private quarters with little trouble. But as he drew close, he found soldiers milling about her door. Not wishing to be observed, he made his way to the second level, which overlooked the lower corridor. Peering down, he had a clear view of the princess's door. As he watched, he saw the king and the queen go into her rooms.

Even so, he waited, hoping the princess would be left alone. But when no one emerged, Fabrizio reluctantly put off his visit and took to casual wandering, wending his way up and down the castello's many corridors. The halls were very crowded.

In time, Fabrizio made his way into the same great hall they had entered when he and Mangus had first arrived. Having no desire to mingle with soldiers, he went among the meager rooms where the servants were quartered. These rooms — there were many — were so congested, it was like a city within the castello. Since few had doors, it was easy to look inside the rooms.

Some of the places were work spaces for carpenters, a chandler, weavers. But other places, by their look, were simply living quarters in which numerous workers appeared to lodge.

There were many people about. Some were working. Others were upon their ease. At first none of them paid any attention to Fabrizio. But, almost always, a second look brought stares of recognition along with a measure of alarm. At first this rather pleased Fabrizio, enjoying the notion that people thought him powerful. It wasn't long, however, before he began to realize it also meant he was noticed no matter where he went.

Still, he wandered on, not looking for anything in particular but allowing his curiosity to examine rooms that were unoccupied. In just such a fashion he came upon the statue.

It was in a living place. Though small, hardly more than a hole in the wall, the room contained four pallets on the floor. Some odd bits of clothing were heaped about. The stone walls were pitted and scarred and bore an extensive jumble of graffiti. There was no window, and only one table. But on this table stood a wooden statue of Our Blessed Lady. Her garments were tinted blue. She was about the right size to have fit into the niche.

Making sure no one was about, Fabrizio went into the room to examine it. From his pocket he took out the wood splinter, the one Mangus had found in the empty niche, and compared its color to the statue's. It was the same.

Carefully, he picked up the statue and turned it about. It had some holes in the back that suggested a bracket had once been attached. Some of the wood around this fastening place had been broken off. It was as if the whole statue had been pulled from the wall.

Fabrizio placed the wood piece that Mangus found into a gash on the wood. It fit exactly.

Elated by his discovery, he was just putting the statue back on the table when he suddenly heard a voice. "Ah, Signore Fabrizio, you like my statue."

Fabrizio spun about. It was Rinaldo, the kitchen boy.

chapter 14

eautiful, isn't it?" Rinaldo said.

"It is," Fabrizio said with discomfort, feeling that Rinaldo always seemed to keep one step ahead of him.

The kitchen boy came farther into the room. "The statue is a consolation to me," he said. "I used to have one like it at home where I slept at night."

"You're lucky to have it," Fabrizio said.

"I am," the boy said, "but you will never — even with all your magic — guess how this one came to be mine."

Fabrizio made a mock bow. "You know what they say," he returned, "'To tell a lie, you must first know the truth.'"

Rinaldo started, but all the same he said, "When I came to the castello — some weeks ago — I didn't work in the kitchen. I cleaned the halls. One day, when sweeping near where the queen has her quarters, she suddenly appeared with that statue. It was she who gave it to me."

"The queen!"

"God's truth," Rinaldo said, crossing himself by way of asserting his honesty. "When she came by, I naturally stood apart. She was just about to go into her rooms when she paused and turned to me. 'Here, boy,' she said. 'Find a proper home for this. It's fallen from its place.'

"I thanked her profusely and I brought the statue here." Rinaldo glanced at it with affection.

Fabrizio stared at the boy in astonishment.

"But what brings you here?" Rinaldo asked in a mocking tone. "What do we have to do to make you our leader?"

Fabrizio drew himself up. "My duty is to Mangus and the noble family."

"Does that include Count Scarazoni?"

"He serves the king."

"And if the king himself is in danger?"

"Do you think he is?"

"Whoever sits on a throne is in danger," Rinaldo parried. "Is that what brought you here?" he asked with sudden scorn. "To tell me of your duty?"

Deciding it would be best to be bold, Fabrizio said, "It was that statue."

"What do you mean?"

"As you told me, Princess Teresina has been haunted by a ghost."

"Did I say that?"

Fabrizio gazed at Rinaldo intently. "You did. Do you know *where* she sees it?"

"How would I know such a thing as that?" Rinaldo replied. He seemed irritated.

"The ghost appears in the niche where that statue used to sit."

Rinaldo began to look uncomfortable. "How do you know?" he demanded.

Fabrizio smiled. "My master has his ways of reasoning."

"I assure you, it was the queen who gave it to me," Rinaldo insisted.

Saying nothing, Fabrizio made his way out of the room.

"Fabrizio!" Rinaldo called after him. "You would be wise to consider me your friend."

Fabrizio, unsure if the boy was threatening him or making an offer of friendship, shrugged and kept walking. It was only after he had gone some way did he realize that he had never told Rinaldo his name. How had he come to know it? As for the story of the queen, that, he was certain, was complete nonsense.

Pondering these things, he was halfway back to Mangus's chamber when he remembered he'd meant to speak to the princess. The question was, should he or should he not tell her he'd been unable to get Mangus to come to the niche that night, as she'd wanted?

As Fabrizio walked on, head bowed, thoughts concentrated on what he should do, a hand reached out to touch him. Startled, he looked up. It was the queen.

Fabrizio made a hasty bow.

"Follow me," she whispered. "I have something important to ask you." She moved away.

Fabrizio, not knowing whether to be alarmed, followed along. She led him down a hall, then up a curling flight of steps, saying no more until she came to a door. "In here," she whispered.

It was the chapel Fabrizio had been in that morning. Still suffused with light from the stained-glass windows on the outside wall, as well as from the green-tinted windows of the inner wall, the chapel smelled strongly of incense. The altar candle was burning.

Fabrizio, head bowed with respect and anxiousness, came forward.

"Last night," the queen said with anger, "you spoke to the princess."

"My lady . . . ," Fabrizio stammered, glancing up so he might see the queen's face the better to judge her thoughts and measure his response accordingly. But she had taken care to keep in shadow. "My lady," Fabrizio went on, "you know what they say: 'When a cat speaks, mice will listen.' It was she who spoke to me."

The queen frowned. "Why were you even about?"

"My master told me to fetch some water."

"Water?"

"I was trying to find the kitchens," Fabrizio said as humbly as he could. "But, begging your pardon, never having been here before, I became lost."

The queen considered his words in silence, then moved restlessly about the chapel. In so doing, she stepped into enough light so that Fabrizio could see more of her face. That she was upset was obvious. But Fabrizio thought he detected something else. Was it fear?

At length, the queen turned toward him again. "I'm perfectly aware," she said, "that, though forbidden to do so, the princess wanders about at night. What did she say to you?"

"My lady, she told me about the ghost she had seen and warned me of the dangers of being alone in the corridors at night."

The queen pursed her lips. Then she said, "Did she tell you if she saw the ghost again?"

Fabrizio took a deep breath. "She did, my lady."

"And you," she asked, "did *you* see it?"

"My lady, it would be wrong for such a one as me — the lowest of the low — to contradict my betters. As they say, 'Truth, like water, flows down.'"

"Yes or no? Did you see it?"

Fabrizio squirmed. How could he say he had seen it when he did not say so to Mangus? He hung his head. "No, my lady, I did not."

The queen gazed at him thoughtfully. At length, she said, "I believe my child is mad."

"*Mad*, my lady!"

"Seeing a ghost is a kind of madness. You were right to humor her."

"Don't you believe her, my lady?" Fabrizio asked.

"It's the king — taken by up magic and superstition — who thinks she speaks the truth."

"My lady," the boy blurted out, "my master says it's all because she doesn't wish to marry."

"Marriage!" the queen cried. "Who spoke of marriage?"

"She did — to him."

The queen turned away.

"With permission," Fabrizio ventured, "is this madness due to her brother's death?"

The queen whirled around to face the boy. "How dare you talk of such a thing!"

Fabrizio backed up. "My lady, the princess told my master she believes the ghost is her brother."

"What else did she say?"

"That he was murdered."

The queen grew very pale. "Who else was present when she said these things?"

"Count Scarazoni."

"What was his reaction?"

"He was not pleased."

After a moment, the queen said, "It may do no harm if the princess befriends you. It may even do her some good. Perhaps she will share more of her thoughts. She is . . . shy of me. And of the king. Naturally, you must report to me what she has said, saying nothing to anyone else. Have no fear, I'll reward you well."

"But, my . . . lady," Fabrizio stammered, hardly knowing how to respond. "I could not be her true friend if she knew I told you everything she said to me."

"Then make sure she does not know. Who better than her mother to protect her?"

"But, with permission, my lady, Mangus is my master. . . ."

"Mangus is a foolish old man. I expressly forbid you to tell him of this conversation. Is that clear?"

Though he said nothing, Fabrizio tried to think of some way to show the queen he could not be ordered about so lightly.

She made a tiny motion with her hand. "Now go. You will hear from me. No, wait! What is your name?"

"Fabrizio, my lady."

"Here, Fabrizio. Take this." The queen held out a delicate hand with a gold coin at her fingertips. "It will seal our bargain."

No sooner did Fabrizio take the coin than he made a simple pass with his hands so that it looked like the coin vanished, holding up both hands to show that it was gone.

The queen was astonished.

"My lady," Fabrizio said, seeking to take

advantage of her confusion, "with your permission, I should like to ask you a question."

The queen, backing away, stared wide-eyed at him. "You may ask," she whispered.

"It's about a statue of Our Blessed Mother, the one in the niche nearest the princess's quarters. Did you take it?"

"How can you know so many things?" she asked, amazed. "It *was* . . . ," she stammered, "old and somewhat broken. It didn't seem right for it to be so near my daughter's rooms. So I removed it and gave it to a servant. Why do you ask?"

"My master wished to know."

The queen stood still for a moment. Then she said, "I must go." She started to move toward the door only to realize Fabrizio was in her way.

Turning, she moved toward the cabinet, the same place that Fabrizio and Rinaldo had passed through to come into the chapel. Pulling the door open, she started to step forward, when she suddenly gave a cry.

Fabrizio rushed to her side. On the floor was the body of Teresina's tutor, Signore Addetto. He was dead.

chapter 15

The queen and Fabrizio stared at the lifeless body.

The queen spoke first. "Leave immediately!" she commanded. "You mustn't be found here."

"But, my lady, you are sure . . . ?"

"Go!"

Fabrizio rushed out of the chapel, then along a corridor. Finding a stairwell, he plunged down until he reached another level. Only then did he pause and try to collect his breath and wits.

Signore Addetto killed. Who could have done such a thing? And why? The first one he thought of was Rinaldo. He had a knife. Then Fabrizio remembered Scarazoni in the carriage. The count kept a blade on his hip, too. For that

matter, he recalled, so did the king. Or perhaps — the thought made the hair at the back of
his neck prickle — it was the ghost who had
done it. Hadn't he heard Addetto admit it was he
who had proposed the murder of the prince, and
that the ghost was seeking revenge?

Fabrizio decided he must tell the princess
what had happened. But, suddenly, he heard
shouts of "Treason!" and "Murder!"

Within moments, soldiers were swarming
everywhere, running toward the chapel. Some
had drawn swords.

Fabrizio flattened himself against the walls to
let them pass.

Once they had done so, he made his way to
where the princess had her chambers. Reaching
the area, he found soldiers milling about her
doors. Afraid of getting too close, he stopped.

But even as he stood there, Count Scarazoni —
along with the king — burst from the girl's
rooms. Surrounded by soldiers, they came running down the corridor. Fabrizio hoped they
would not notice him, but he was not successful.

"You there, boy!" It was Count Scarazoni
calling.

Fabrizio had no choice but to step forward.
"Yes, my lord."

The king, his hand on his hip dagger, was in a nervous sweat. He kept looking up and down the corridor, as if in search — and fear — of something.

"Where is your master?" the count demanded.

"In his room, my lord, reasoning."

"He's reasoned enough," Scarazoni snapped. "Appalling things are happening. The princess's tutor has been slain."

"The spies have struck," the king cried. "Something must be done!"

Scarazoni waved the soldiers away. Then he drew close to Fabrizio. "Has your master come to some sort of conclusion?" he asked.

"My lord, it's not for me to say."

"Tell him haste is crucial!" the king barked. "I must have this resolved."

Fabrizio, desperate to find some way to help his master, made a decision. "My lord, with permission, he did ask —"

"Ask what?"

"He . . . he wishes to go into the corridors tonight to stand watch at the place where the princess saw her visions."

"Excellent!" Scarazoni cried. "My lord," he said to the king, "this should clear up the matter once and for all. It's the wisest thing to do."

The sweat stood out on the king's brow. "Tell Mangus he has our permission," he said. "Will he come alone? Does he wish guards?"

Fabrizio thought as fast as he could. "Just he and I, my lord. And, with permission, the princess."

The king wrung his hands but finally said, "Yes, yes, that's wise."

"At what time?" Scarazoni asked.

"Midnight, my lord," Fabrizio replied.

"So be it! Now, my lord," the count said to the king, "Addetto . . ." The two men — with their guards — hurried away, leaving Fabrizio alone in the hall. For a moment he watched them go, then he turned, more resolved than ever to approach the princess.

After making certain the hall was deserted, Fabrizio approached the door to the princess's rooms and knocked.

The door opened a crack. An eye observed him. The next moment, the door pulled open, and a hand reached out and pulled him inside.

"Bravo, Fabrizio!" Teresina cried, drawing him farther into the room and shutting the door. "To come so boldly. How like you. Last night when I returned, I prayed fervently that you be kept well. Don't worry," she added as she latched her door, "if someone comes, I have a place to hide you. Did you bring news?"

Fabrizio glanced about her chamber. The walls were covered by tapestries depicting flowers, knights, and ladies. Her canopied bed, narrow and high, was piled with comforters and pillows. A dressing table laden with jewels and multicolored bottles was set against one wall. A large trunk stood next to another. Candles provided light.

"Teresina," Fabrizio said, "something dreadful has happened."

"Why . . . what?"

"Your tutor, Signore Addetto, has been murdered."

Teresina made a face. "Has he? I suppose I should be sorry about it, but I didn't like him. He was always trying to get me to do what the count wanted. Fabrizio, he was the count's man. You needn't worry."

"But before that happened, I overheard a conversation between Scarazoni and him."

"Oh, clever Fabrizio!" Teresina cried, clapping her hands with joy. "Tell me everything they said."

Fabrizio told her. When he was done, he

asked, "Teresina, how much of that did you know?"

"Why, all of it," she said, seemingly surprised at his question.

"*All?*"

"Of course. Except, I'm quite certain my brother was not just killed but murdered."

"But who would do such a thing?" Fabrizio cried, taken aback by the girl's almost cheerful reaction.

"Count Scarazoni," she answered.

"And Addetto?"

"The same. Scarazoni's very cruel. But what about Mangus?" Teresina asked. "Will he come to view the niche?"

"My lady, at midnight tonight, I think he'll go to the place where the ghost appears."

"Bravo, Fabrizio!" the princess enthused.

"I'll be there with him. And you, too, for that matter."

The princess beamed. "Good for you, Fabrizio. Oh, I do love these intrigues so."

"Princess," Fabrizio said, "according to Mangus, it's a matter of grave seriousness. And your tutor . . . remember, he is dead."

"I will pray for his soul," the girl said. "But,

Fabrizio, what did you think of my interview with your master? Didn't I play the game exceedingly well?"

"What game?"

"The deception game. And, Fabrizio, I did another clever thing. I told my mother that you and I met in the halls last night."

"Why did you do that?"

"She insists I confide in her. To keep her happy, I tell her secrets. Some are true. Some are not. Fabrizio, I may be only ten, but I've learned one thing: To make a conspiracy work, you must mix truth with falseness.

"As for tonight," she went on, "I'm very pleased Mangus will stand watch. It's exactly what I wanted. When the ghost appears, your master will see that it is real and so advise my father. Then the marriage will not take place."

"But, Teresina . . . what if the ghost does not come?"

The princess became serious. "We can only pray it does."

There was a sudden rapping on the door.

"Princess!" came a woman's voice. "I have returned."

"My new lady-in-waiting!" the princess whispered. "She mustn't know you're here. She tells Scarazoni everything. This way! Quickly!"

She rushed to the wall behind the bed, lifted up a corner of the tapestry, and revealed a door, which she opened.

"Here, take this," she said, thrusting a lighted candle into Fabrizio's hand. "Go down the steps. At the bottom, you'll come out into a corridor. From there you can find your own way."

Fabrizio had little choice. With the woman knocking harder, insisting she be allowed to enter, he darted into the passageway. But when the door slammed shut behind him, it made enough wind to blow the candle out.

Standing in total darkness, Fabrizio listened as Teresina and her lady made idle chatter. Once again he marveled at how changeable Teresina was, a real actor.

Remembering his danger, he put his mind to matters at hand.

When he had leaped out of the room, he'd managed to see a flight of steps that led downward. Now that he was in complete darkness, it was necessary to feel his way to the top step.

No sooner did he reach the first step than he heard sounds coming from the stairwell below. It sounded as if someone was going down.

With a jolt, Fabrizio realized that the person — whoever it was — must have been listening to his conversation with the princess. He must find out who had been there.

He began to move down. More than once he caught himself from falling. Then — from how far below, he could not tell — he heard a door slam. The meaning was clear: The person he was pursuing had escaped.

Fabrizio continued down until he came against a wall. Feeling about, he found a door. He pushed and found himself in a corridor. Not a soul was in sight. But, a few steps from the door, he noticed a glove on the ground. Fabrizio picked it up. The glove was black leather, with yellow trim. Count Scarazoni's glove.

Did that mean it was Count Scarazoni who had been listening? Or was it only someone who had wished him to think it was the count?

Fabrizio stuffed the glove into his pocket and started back to Mangus, only to realize he'd completely forgotten to ask the princess about the statue.

chapter 16

As soon as Fabrizio returned to Mangus, he informed his master what he had learned about the statue. "It was in the servants' quarters. A kitchen boy had it."

"How did he come by it?"

"He claimed the queen gave it to him."

Mangus's eyes opened wide with surprise. "Do you think that's true?"

Not knowing how he could talk about the queen without talking about the princess, Fabrizio merely shrugged.

Mangus said, "Perhaps the statue has no significance to our quest."

"Master, I have other news."

"Tell me."

"Signore Addetto has been murdered."

"Murdered!"

"I'm afraid so, Master."

Mangus gave a deep sigh and made the sign of the cross. "Poor soul," he murmured. "He wished to speak to me."

"You know what they say, Master: 'Least said, most spoken.' What do you think he wanted to say?"

Mangus smoothed his beard with his fingers. "I don't know. But I regret telling Scarazoni he had wished to meet me."

"Do you think the count killed Addetto?"

"All I know, Fabrizio, is that our lives are very much in danger."

"The king said he must have your conclusions soon."

Mangus shook his head. "Signore Addetto's fate suggests that he is right." Head bowed, he fell into a reverie.

"Master," Fabrizio blurted out, "Count Scarazoni wants you to go to the niche tonight to look for the ghost."

"Does he?"

"He . . . does, Master," Fabrizio lied. "You're to be there at the hour of midnight."

"Well, then, I will."

Fabrizio, feeling guilt at his fabrication, averted his eyes.

They ate their supper in silence. "I must try to make sense of this all," Mangus explained.

Fabrizio did not protest. He had learned so many things — only some of which he had told Mangus — that he had an abundance of his own puzzles to solve. Besides, he was fearful he would blurt out his lie and make things worse.

At one point, however, he could not help saying, "Master, with permission, may I ask a question?"

"Anything you wish."

"We have only a day or two to solve this mystery, is that correct?"

"That seems to be the case."

"What if we don't solve it within the appointed time?"

"Count Scarazoni will find an excuse to kill me."

"But, why?"

"Men of power — like Scarazoni — do not like their weaknesses known."

"What is his weakness, Master?"

"He needs me."

"Why should that matter?"

"Ah, Fabrizio, as for that, my years have

taught me that he who has power has merely taught others they have none."

"But what about me, Signore?" Fabrizio cried. "I know as much of this affair as you." And he thought, but did not say, *I know even more.*

"Why, Fabrizio, surely you understood. If Scarazoni learns how much you know, your life will be forfeit, too."

"Me?" Fabrizio cried out in alarm.

"Ah, Fabrizio, I warned you, did I not?"

Fabrizio could eat no more. He was beginning to grasp what he had done. If the ghost came tonight and Mangus saw it and acknowledged it, his own life would be in peril.

"Master," he said anxiously, "I've come to a different conclusion than I had before. May I say what I think?"

"Please."

"If you see the ghost and say it is real, the marriage will be put off and Count Scarazoni will do you harm. But if you say there is no ghost, the marriage will take place and Count Scarazoni will usurp the king but set you free."

"Perhaps. But, Fabrizio, you may be certain, no ghost will come."

"But if it *does* come, Master," Fabrizio cried, his eyes suddenly ripe with tears, "and your reason tells you it is there, you will proclaim your own death. Either way, great trouble will come."

"That is true."

"Master, forgive me. I think it's better to be a living donkey than a dead wise man. Just say there is no ghost."

Mangus looked at the boy reproachfully. "Fabrizio, I warned you, I must speak the truth as I see it."

Fabrizio said no more but spent the evening covering his nervousness by practicing coin tricks, much to Mangus's annoyance.

At length there came a sharp rapping on the door. Mangus, on the bed, had been dozing. Fabrizio was just about to open the door when Mangus whispered, "Be careful, Fabrizio. Be *very* careful."

The boy nodded his understanding.

It was Count Scarazoni. A sword was on one hip, a stiletto on his other. In his hand he held a lantern. He wore no gloves. Fabrizio suddenly remembered he had the count's glove in his pocket. But it was too late to do anything about it.

"The king is waiting," Scarazoni announced. "I'm glad you requested doing this," he added.

Mangus looked around. "Did I?" he said.

"Your boy brought me your request."

"Ah, yes," Mangus said, darting a glance at Fabrizio.

The boy looked away.

The trio made their way along the stone corridors. Scarazoni scowled but did not speak. Mangus, chilly despite the thick and sultry air, pulled up his hood and was clasping his gloved hands within his sleeves like a monk. Fabrizio was sure he was praying.

The previous night — when he searched for water — Fabrizio had seen almost no one in the halls. This night no one was to be seen, either. But there was a difference — a deep, unnatural quiet. Despite the heat, it made him shudder.

They soon came to the meeting place, the empty niche. To Fabrizio's eyes, it was the same as the night before. This time, however, the king was waiting with Teresina. She was dressed in a loose white gown, festooned with pearls. On her head was a close-fitting cap. Silver-colored slippers were on her feet. Her manner was as Fabrizio had first beheld her — rigid, showing no emotion, eyes cast down, hands clasped.

The thought came to Fabrizio that he really didn't know who the princess truly was. Was she the person he saw before him, or the one he saw privately?

"God be with you," Mangus said, and bowed.

"God be with us," the king returned. His voice shook.

The king, like Scarazoni, was armed with sword and dagger. His sweating brow, and agitated hands — busy clasping and unclasping the hilt of his blade — suggested just how nervous he was. His small eyes could not stay still but kept darting glances at Mangus, then turning away.

Fabrizio wondered if one of the daggers — the king's or Scarazoni's — had slain Addetto.

Count Scarazoni said, "There are guards at each end of the corridor. No one will be allowed to come into this area on pain of death."

"Then we must leave," the king said, anxious to get away. "It's close to midnight."

"My lord," Mangus said. "With permission, may I ask a question?"

"Ask."

"If there is a ghost, will the marriage not take place?"

"How do you know about the marriage?" the king demanded.

"The princess informed me."

The king glanced at Scarazoni, who nodded.

"I have studied the stars," the king said. "The only propitious time for her to marry is two days from now. If not then, two years must elapse."

"Very well," Mangus said. "Now, my lords, with your permission, I must respectfully request that you leave us alone."

Scarazoni withdrew.

The king made the sign of the cross over his daughter's brow and moved off, too, only to pause and say, "The boy?"

"Ah, well," Mangus said with a show of indifference. "He'd best stay."

"We'll not be far," the king said, and moved away. "If the need arises, call."

Fabrizio heard the clicking of his heels on the stone floors as he went.

"Good," Mangus said softly. "We are alone." He made a bow to the princess. "My lady, I'm glad to see you again."

Teresina gave a slight nod of her head, no more.

Fabrizio wondered if he detected some triumphant glitter to her eye. Or was it only the reflection of a burning lamp?

"Princess," Mangus said, "I must tell you truthfully, I do not expect to see this thing."

"Why not?"

"I don't believe it exists."

"It does."

"Then you agree with the boy who arranged that we meet here tonight. Well, we shall see. Fabrizio, put out the lights."

A chagrined Fabrizio did as told. All became dim. It was hard for him to know where the little light remaining came from. Perhaps, he thought, from the higher windows.

"Let us be silent," Mangus said.

Mangus and the princess stood opposite the niche, against the wall, eyes fixed to the place. Fabrizio stood a little farther off, watching both of them and, with a slight turn of his head, the spot.

It became deathly still. Now and again, from somewhere, a dog barked. Once, a bat fluttered by, and an owl hooted. No more. As time passed, the silence became even more intense.

Waiting, Fabrizio hardly knew what he wanted to happen. One moment he wanted the ghost to appear, so Mangus might admit it existed. The next moment he wished it would not appear, fearful that if Mangus pronounced the ghost had come, Scarazoni would kill them both.

From a distance, bells began to toll. Fabrizio, beginning to sweat, counted the strokes, twelve peals in all. It was midnight.

Across the way, the princess was staring steadily at the niche. Mangus, too, was gazing fixedly in the same direction.

Suddenly, the princess gave a sharp intake of breath. "Look!" she cried. She was pointing to the wall.

Fabrizio looked up. There, without question, rather high, was the faint green glow. Even as he looked, it was growing brighter as well as moving downward — as though from heaven itself.

"It's come!" Teresina said in a hushed if urgent voice. She took a step away from Mangus.

Head cocked to one side, Mangus was staring wide-eyed at the light. The green, blurry brightness had now fixed itself within the niche. The form had head, arms, and torso, which moved. Fabrizio had no doubt: It was like the writhing shadow of a lost and tormented soul.

"Do you see it?" Fabrizio heard the princess say.

"I see something," Mangus said cautiously.

"It's the ghost," the princess whispered. "And there, you see, he is beckoning."

"Does it speak?" Mangus asked. His voice had become low, strained.

"Not yet."

"Speak to it," he whispered urgently. "Make it speak so I may hear."

"Talk to me," Teresina called, her voice barely more than a moan. "Talk to me."

Suddenly, Mangus took a step forward and cried, "If you be something intelligible, speak so we may know your needs!"

Though very frightened, Fabrizio kept his eyes on the ghost. It seemed now sharply defined, now a fuzzy haze.

Mangus took another step forward. "Shadow!" he called. "Be you something of this earth or do you come from some other, nether world? Speak so we may know your desire!"

And then — not attached to any form or shape Fabrizio could see but coming as if from some other, distant place — a voice did come.

"I was murdered . . ." the voice said in distinct words. "Murdered by Scarazoni's hand." No sooner were the words spoken than the thing began to fade away.

Fabrizio was terrified.

"I hear you," Mangus cried. "But what do you wish?"

"I wish —"

"Say it!"

"I wish . . . I wish . . . to be avenged. Avenged by the magician's boy."

chapter 17

Heart fluttering, Fabrizio stared at the apparition, unable to believe what he was hearing and seeing.

Teresina — eyes closed, hands clasped as though in prayer — was standing halfway between Mangus and the ghost. "What do you want of the magician's boy?" she asked loudly.

"He . . . is . . . needed," the voice intoned.

"To do what?"

"He alone has the power to avenge my death," said the voice. Having spoken these words, the vision began to fade until only darkness remained where light had been.

Weak limbed, finding it hard to breathe,

shivering as though ill, Fabrizio leaned back against the wall.

Suddenly, the princess gave a cry of fright and fell into Mangus's arms.

"Lights! Lights!" Mangus cried. "My lords! My lords! Hurry! Help!"

The king and Scarazoni came rushing down the corridor. Scarazoni had his sword drawn. King Claudio, a step behind, held a lantern high in one hand. In his other hand was an unsheathed blade.

"What's happened?" Scarazoni called out. "What is it?"

"Did it come?" the king shouted. Then he saw the princess in Mangus's arms. "My daughter!" he cried. Knife and lantern clattered to the floor as he snatched the girl from Mangus. "Teresina!" he cried. "Teresina!"

"Is she dead?" Scarazoni asked, looking over his shoulder. His sword was pointed right at Mangus.

Fabrizio was too frightened to do anything but gape at the scene before him.

The king put an ear to the princess's heart. "She lives," he said with great relief. "She lives!"

"What was it?" Scarazoni demanded of Mangus, his sword dimpling Mangus's robe.

"My lord, it was . . . something," Mangus gasped. He was craning his neck, looking about the corridor, up, down, around, in every direction.

"*Something?*" a livid Scarazoni cried, grabbing hold of Mangus's robe at the throat and shoving the old man hard against the wall. "What do you mean? Tell me what you saw!"

"It was what the princess said," Mangus managed to say. "Something like a ghost."

"*Like* a ghost? What does that mean? Was it a ghost or not?"

"My lord, I don't know," Mangus gasped, trying to free himself from Scarazoni's grip.

The king hovered over his daughter, talking to her, rubbing her hands.

Fabrizio was being ignored. While he saw all that was happening, he was too panicked to think with clarity. He kept hearing the ghost's words, that it had been murdered, that it could only be avenged by *his* destroying Scarazoni!

Then he heard Scarazoni demand of Mangus, "Did the thing have a voice?"

"Please, let me go, my lord," Mangus cried. "You are . . . hurting me. I cannot . . . speak."

"Answer me!" Scarazoni shouted as he thrust his face close to the old man. "What did the thing *do?*"

"Nothing," Mangus gasped. "It was just . . . there."

"What happened to the princess?"

"She called out to it, then fainted. That's when I called for help."

"Then it's true," Fabrizio heard the king say. "There is a ghost. You see, Scarazoni, my daughter did not lie." Lowering Teresina to the floor, he rubbed her hands and patted her cheeks, trying to bring her back to consciousness. "Fetch the queen!" he shouted to a soldier.

The man ran off.

"She's opening her eyes," the king announced.

All attention went to the princess.

"It's gone," the king was saying to her. "Gone, my love. You are safe."

Count Scarazoni knelt before the girl. "Did it speak, princess? Did it speak?"

She nodded briefly.

"What did it say?" Scarazoni asked.

Mangus edged forward to hear the girl's reply.

Teresina blinked open her eyes, gazed at Scarazoni, and cried, "It is my brother's ghost! My brother has been murdered!" Sobbing, she sat up and threw herself into her father's arms.

Furious, Scarazoni reached out toward her,

only to have the king strike his hand away. "Leave her alone!" he snapped. It was the first time Fabrizio had heard him speak harshly to Scarazoni.

Taken by surprise, Scarazoni backed away.

The queen came running down the corridor, her loose hair streaming behind her. Seeing the princess on the floor with her father, she came to a sudden halt. Then, with a swooning cry of fright, she knelt and threw her arms about her daughter, calling to her.

With all the attention on the girl, Fabrizio had time to recover his own senses. He had heard the ghost speak, saying that it had been murdered by Scarazoni, that it wanted him to seek revenge. Yet it had said nothing as to who it was — even as Teresina claimed it was her brother.

Fabrizio stared at the group huddled about the princess. Just behind Count Scarazoni was Mangus. It took Fabrizio a moment to realize his master was looking right at him. Their eyes met.

Mangus raised a finger to his lips, giving a clear indication that Fabrizio was to say nothing. The boy was in no mind to disobey.

But he did do something. Fearful that at any moment the ghost's words would be made known, and that he might be in Scarazoni's hands, Fabrizio slipped the count's glove from his pocket and flipped it as far as he could. It landed on the floor just below the niche.

The king and queen, meanwhile, had taken up their daughter and bore her toward her chambers. The soldiers followed.

Mangus, Fabrizio, and Scarazoni remained. They watched the princess go. When she was gone, Scarazoni swung about.

"If you value your life, Mangus," he said, "you will tell me everything that happened. The truth, now!"

"My lord," Mangus began, fairly well composed, though he kept rubbing his hands, "you will recall you left us shortly before midnight while we waited here before this niche. Not long after the hour of midnight struck, a light began to appear upon the wall."

"A ghost?"

"My lord, with permission, hear me out. The light moved until it found its way to the niche. I could see that within this light was a shadowy human form. Head, arms, torso."

"Then you do believe it was a ghost," Scarazoni said with anger.

"My lord," Mangus returned with exasperation, "I do not know what it was!"

"Did it make threatening motions?" Scarazoni demanded. "Did it speak, make itself known by name in any way? Why did the princess say it was her brother?"

"It did make motions, my lord," Mangus replied. "And I observed the princess calling to it. But . . . but whether it spoke or not to her — I, at least . . . I did not hear."

Fabrizio, startled to hear his master lie, looked at him with amazement.

"As for it being her brother," Mangus continued, "I hardly know what to say. Is he truly dead?"

Instead of answering the question, Scarazoni glared at the old man. "Mangus, what do you think she saw?"

"My lord, with permission," Mangus said with great weariness, "I do not believe in ghosts."

"You are useless!" Scarazoni said, and lifted his arm as though to strike. Even as he did, Fabrizio leaped forward before the blow, which, when it came, struck him down.

"Fabrizio!" Mangus cried.

"Stupid boy!" Scarazoni bellowed, and whirled

about. Then he stopped. As he saw his glove upon the stones, his anger drained away. With effort, he went forward and took up the glove as if it were some odious thing. "Where did this come from?" he demanded in a trembling voice. "I have been searching for it."

"For what, my lord?" Mangus asked.

"This glove!"

"I know nothing about a glove, my lord."

"Mangus," Scarazoni whispered in a voice shaking with rage, "you have one day to get rid of this so-called ghost or you shall become a ghost yourself!" With this pronouncement, the count whirled about and stormed away, shouting, "Put them back in their chamber! Put them back!"

Soldiers appeared, gathering around Mangus and Fabrizio. In haste, the two were escorted back to their chamber, where they were all but thrown inside.

Mangus guided Fabrizio to the bed, where he insisted the boy lie down. Sitting beside him, he patted his hand. "My boy, are you all right?" he asked gently.

Fabrizio tried to sit up. "Master . . ."

Mangus restrained him. "Fabrizio, you came

between me and that brute. He would have hurt me badly. I owe you many thanks."

"Master," Fabrizio said, "I heard the ghost speak."

"Fabrizio," Mangus said as firmly as ever, "there are no such things as ghosts."

Tears fell from Fabrizio's eyes. "But, Master," he cried, "I heard you say you saw it. And when it spoke, you responded."

"I willingly admit I heard and saw *something*," Mangus replied. "But, Fabrizio," he added fiercely, "there must be some reasoned explanation."

"Master," Fabrizio pleaded, "the thing said it was murdered by Scarazoni, that it wished *me* to avenge him. What am I to do?"

Mangus shook his head. "I don't know," he admitted. "There's much here I don't understand."

"Why did you tell the count you didn't hear the ghost speak?" Fabrizio whispered. "Why did you — who never lie — tell an untruth?"

"It is a sin, I know. But . . . I admit, I feared for my life. Fabrizio, there is a conspiracy afoot in this castello. We are surrounded by it. Sometimes I think you are part of it."

"Me!"

"Fabrizio, it was you who arranged that I visit the niche, was it not?"

Fabrizio nodded.

"Why?"

"Forgive me, Master. I . . . I wanted you to see the ghost."

Frustrated, Mangus closed his eyes. *"Reason,"* he said fervently. *"Reason."*

Fabrizio, much subdued, asked, "Master, what will happen now?"

Mangus shook his head. "I must find out how and why that light and voice came to be there. It must be some deception."

"Deception!" Fabrizio cried.

"Yes, a hoax," Mangus said with force.

"Master, with permission, did you not say that to deny what one sees with one's own eyes is a form of madness?"

The old man remained still, lost in thought. Then he murmured, as much to himself as to Fabrizio, "I wish I could look at that place again."

"Master," said Fabrizio, remembering his promise to the princess that he would go to her after the visitation. "Let me go to look for you."

The old man shook his head. "No, it's too dangerous."

"I'm here to serve you, Master. Just tell me what you wish me to see for you."

"Fabrizio," Mangus said, "you heard the voice, did you not?"

"Yes, Master."

"And the princess said she heard it, too."

"Yes, Master."

"And so did I," Mangus said without apology. "But Fabrizio," he continued, "mark me, she chose not to reveal *all* of what the voice said when asked by Count Scarazoni. Why? It was as if the voice was meant to be heard by another. Who?"

"I don't know, Master."

"And yet it was to you it spoke."

Fabrizio felt ill.

"That light, Fabrizio," Mangus continued, "that voice had to come from somewhere. I must find it."

Fabrizio went to the door and opened it. "Master, they haven't locked us in. I'll go and look at the niche for you." He was glad for the excuse to leave.

Mangus cocked his head to one side. "Is there another reason you wish to go?"

"Oh, no, Master! I'm no more than a finger to your hand."

"Are you quite sure?"

"Oh, Master, how could you even think otherwise?"

Mangus sighed. "Go, then, but be very cautious and return quickly." Turning toward the portrait of the Blessed Martyr, Saint Stephano, so pierced with arrows, he knelt, pressed his hands over his beard, and began to pray.

Fabrizio backed away. For a moment he hesitated, all but blurting out all the things he had not said, that everything he was doing was all for his master's benefit. But fearful of making things worse, he left the room.

chapter 18

F abrizio ran along the empty corridors toward the princess's chambers. Suddenly he
stopped. Troubled by Mangus's suggestion that
he had not been completely loyal, he was determined to go by the ghostly niche and do as he'd
promised.

As Fabrizio crept around the last corner that
led to the niche, he caught sight of a fluttering
light at the far end of the hall. Alarmed, he
darted back around the bend, then stole a peek
to see who or what was there.

Someone, hooded lamp in hand, was standing
before the niche. Keeping close to the walls,
Fabrizio crept forward, trusting the darkness

would conceal him. He looked again. It was Count Scarazoni, standing in deep thought.

Fascinated, Fabrizio watched. The count appeared to be doing nothing but staring at the niche while fingering his glove. He knelt and lifted his hands in prayer. Then he rose, went forward, and placed his hand into the niche, as if to feel about the space. Finally, he turned about and, with head bowed, began to walk in Fabrizio's direction.

The boy had been so engrossed, he was caught off guard. Spinning about, he raced down the hall, took the first turn, then plunged up a flight of steps, reached another level, then sped around yet another bend.

"Wait! Boy! Stop!" came a high-pitched cry from behind him. Fabrizio ran even faster.

As he reached the end of a corridor, a white form — like some phantom — leaped before him, blocking his way. Fabrizio stopped in his tracks. It was Teresina. She was holding open a door in the wall.

"In here!" she cried. Fabrizio plunged in. The girl followed, shutting the door behind them.

They had entered a tiny room with a bench, upon which sat a lighted candle. Teresina blew it out, bringing total darkness. Within moments they heard footsteps patter past the door, then fade away.

"Who was chasing you?" Teresina asked.

Fabrizio, panting from fright and exertion, said, "Scarazoni, I think."

"Well, then, he's gone."

"How did you know I would be coming here?" Fabrizio asked.

"Fabrizio," she said, "didn't you say you would come? I believe in you completely."

"Forgive me for taking so long," he said. "Are you all right?"

"Why should I not be all right?" she said as she relit the candle with a flint.

"When the ghost came . . . and spoke . . . you fainted quite away."

Teresina put her hand over her mouth and giggled.

Fabrizio gazed at the girl. She was completely different from the last time he had seen her. Then, she had seemed near death. Now she was bursting with energy.

"Fabrizio, you should trust me more. I only wanted to *look* as if I were about to die. It was a way of bringing my father back."

"Why did you want to do that?"

"So Mangus could tell him he had seen the ghost."

"Teresina," he stammered, "I . . . don't understand."

"Fabrizio, the most important thing is that your master now believes in the ghost."

"Teresina, he still insists it is some trick."

The princess looked at him with concern. "Do you agree with him?" she asked.

"Oh, no," Fabrizio assured her. "The ghost is real. I'd proclaim it anywhere."

"Then you saw and heard it speak?" she said.

"I fear I did," he said.

"Why should you say 'fear,' Fabrizio?"

"Teresina, it . . . called upon *me* to avenge a murder."

"Oh, Fabrizio, what an honor for you!" she exclaimed. "My brother's ghost — heir to the ancient throne Pergamontio — calling upon you to free the kingdom from the tyranny under which it has fallen. You should be thrilled that he selected you to do a great deed. You'll be a hero."

"But, how?"

"By getting Mangus to say there is a ghost. Fabrizio," Teresina pressed, "we have put our trust in you and your magic."

"Who is 'we'?"

For a moment, Teresina seemed at a loss. Then she said, "Why ... all of Pergamontio, goose."

Fabrizio felt like bursting into tears. "Teresina, I'm just a servant. I fear it's true what they say. 'A beast of burden never has enough legs.'"

"You're much too modest. Don't deny your gifts. Though poor and low, you have a majestic soul. I assure you, Fabrizio, you're fated for greatness!"

Fabrizio could only hang his head.

"May I remind you, though," the princess said, "we have only a little time. If you don't hurry, I'll be married and lost."

"But I shall be lost, too!" he cried.

"How so?"

"Mangus says that he and I will live only if you marry. If you don't, our lives will be forfeit."

Teresina looked at him severely. "Fabrizio, have you forgotten your vow of loyalty so soon? You promised to dedicate your life to me."

Fabrizio looked up. There were tears in his eyes.

She placed a hand on his arm. "Dear Fabrizio, I forgive your momentary weakness. It is charming.

But just think, when you have achieved everything, I shall reveal your role and raise you up to a high position. Even if you should die, think how many will pray for your soul!"

Fabrizio groaned.

"Now come," she said. "Be brave. I'll take you back to your chamber so you can think what to do next."

Through one secret passage after another, Teresina led him back toward Mangus's chamber.

Her last words were, "Remember, Fabrizio, all depends upon your convincing Mangus that the ghost was real. Don't worry. I'll find a way to keep you safe."

With those words, she went off.

Watching her go, Fabrizio sighed. It was all too much for him to keep within himself. Then and there, he decided to tell Mangus about his meetings with the princess.

So resolved, he entered the chamber. The candle was all but guttered. Even so, there was light enough to see that Mangus was not there.

chapter 19

Picking over the remnants of their supper, Fabrizio tried to puzzle out where Mangus might be. For all the boy knew, he had simply gone to the latrines.

But as time went by and his master did not return, Fabrizio decided that something was amiss and he needed to look for him. But Mangus could be anywhere. Perhaps he was in a dungeon, or an angry Count Scarazoni might have done him harm.

Remembering the old saying "To open a door, better small coins than a large fist," Fabrizio made sure he had some money in his pocket. Then he left the chamber.

There was no soldier at the door, which

Fabrizio now took to be a bad sign. Once in the hallways, he tried to decide where to go. Perhaps Mangus had grown impatient and gone to see the niche himself. Fabrizio decided to check.

Though he tried to walk softly, Fabrizio's steps seemed to echo loudly. Never had the castello seemed so dark, so empty to him.

As he approached the niche, he moved with increased caution. He had no desire to come upon anyone else the way he had Count Scarazoni.

Upon reaching the final corner, Fabrizio stopped and peeked about the wall. Sure enough, someone was standing motionless in the corridor, facing the niche. A little oil lamp on the ground gave off sufficient light for him to see that the person was neither Scarazoni nor Mangus. It was Queen Jovanna.

Fabrizio was undecided whether to stay or flee. He must find Mangus. Perhaps the queen had seen him. When he reminded himself that the queen had given him permission to address her, he went forward, with just enough noise to alert her to his presence.

Starting with surprise, the queen peered through the dark to see who was approaching.

"My lady," Fabrizio said, feeling obliged to keep his voice low, "with permission, it's me, Fabrizio. The magician's boy."

"Ah!" she said with evident relief. "You startled me. How did you know I was here?"

"My lady, I didn't. My master has disappeared. I thought he might be here. Have you seen him?"

Jovanna contemplated Fabrizio for a moment, then turned away to gaze at the niche again. "I'm sure he's fine," she said.

Not sure what to do, Fabrizio waited.

After a while — though she did not look at him — the queen said, "Fabrizio, did Mangus see the ghost when it came tonight?"

"My lady, he will only say that he saw *something.*"

"And he will admit to no more?"

"My lady, he does not think it was a ghost."

"And you, what did you see?"

"What I saw was not of this world."

"Did the ghost speak?"

Fabrizio hesitated.

"Did it?"

"Yes, my lady."

"What did it say?"

"I'm . . . I'm not sure."

"And afterward, when you met with the princess, what did *she* say to you?"

Fabrizio was too surprised to say anything.

"Don't be alarmed I know," the queen said. "After the coming of the ghost, the king and I brought the princess to her bed. I, in agreement with my husband, placed myself in a private passageway right outside her sleeping room."

Fabrizio thought immediately of the person who had been listening when he'd spoken to the princess in her chamber. Was it, after all, the queen who had been there?

"When I heard her slip from her bed," the queen continued, "I followed, but she eluded me. Only the prince knows the secret passages of this castello better than Teresina. I supposed she took one of them. Then I saw you in the corridor and called on you to stop. You refused."

Fabrizio blinked. So it was the queen, not Scarazoni, who had called after him.

"When you vanished so abruptly," the queen continued, "I was certain the princess had led you away. Why did you run from me?"

"I did not know it was you, my lady. I had just seen Count Scarazoni. I thought it was he, and I was fearful."

The queen gazed at him. "I will believe you," she said, but in such a way that Fabrizio could not tell if she truly did.

After a moment she said, "I asked you to keep me informed about my daughter. What did she say to you?"

Fabrizio hesitated.

"Have no fear," the queen pressed. "I will pay you well."

Fabrizio struggled to find something to say that would not betray the princess. "My lady, she thinks the ghost is your son. With permission, do you think he was murdered?"

"I have very little doubt."

"Who would kill him?"

"Scarazoni," the queen said sadly. Her face seemed old and very tired.

"My lady," Fabrizio said, "if you believe this, why does not the king punish the count?"

The queen made a dismissive gesture with her hand. "The king, my husband, is frightened of many things. Count Scarazoni is the real power here."

"My lady, the king became very angry with Scarazoni tonight."

"Would that he did so more often," the queen said.

"With permission," Fabrizio pressed, "do you now believe it is a ghost your daughter has seen?"

"I do," she said mournfully. "And though it must be very frightful, I should like to behold it."

The two were standing before the niche. The queen had her back toward it. Fabrizio was facing it. No sooner did the queen speak of her desire to see the ghost than Fabrizio observed a green glow upon the wall.

"What is it? What's the matter?" the queen cried, seeing the look of shock on his face.

"My lady," Fabrizio whispered, *"look!"*

The queen turned and gasped.

As the two stood and watched, the green light began to grow in brightness. Gradually, within the glow, a shadowy form appeared.

"The ghost . . . ," Fabrizio managed to say.

The arms of the phantom began to move, as did its head. Fabrizio was sure it was going to speak, but it did not. Instead, the shadowy form seemed to melt, and then disappeared.

"My lady, did you see it?" Fabrizio whispered.

"I did," she whispered. "I must go to the chapel and pray," she said in a weak voice. She started off, but faltered. "Lead me there. I am all atremble." She held out a hand for support.

"My lady, I don't know the way."

"I'll guide you," she said. "It's right above us."

The chapel was, as the queen had said, on the next level, above where they had been. They reached it quickly, meeting no one on the way.

At the doorway the queen said, "Wait for me here. I prefer to be alone."

She opened the door. Standing on the threshold, she peered into the chapel. But instead of going forward, she turned back to Fabrizio. She appeared more agitated than ever. "It is . . . very empty," she said. "I wish you to accompany me."

Fabrizio followed her into the room. The sole light came from the scant altar flame. The smell of melted wax filled the air. Remembering that this was the place where Signore Addetto's body had been found, Fabrizio made the sign of the cross over his heart.

The queen took her hand from Fabrizio's arm and moved forward toward the altar. Suddenly she gasped.

"My lady!" he cried. "What is it?"

In a broken voice, she said, "Boy! Come . . . quickly! There . . . there is . . . another body here."

Fabrizio rushed forward. In a glance he saw who lay upon the floor: It was Mangus.

chapter 20

Horrified, the queen stepped back. Fabrizio dropped to his knees. "Master!" he cried over the body.

"Is he dead?" the queen asked in a strained voice.

Fabrizio put his ear to Mangus's chest. There were heartbeats. "He's alive!" he cried. "Bring light! Hurry!"

The queen snatched up a lighted taper and held it over the old man.

"Master!" Fabrizio called, trying to bring Mangus back to consciousness by rubbing his hands.

Mangus's eyes fluttered open. When he saw the bright candlelight, he blinked once, twice, then put up his hand to shield his eyes. "Ah, Fabrizio," he said, "it's you. I was worried about you. You were gone so long."

"Master," Fabrizio asked, "are you hurt?"

"Hurt?" Mangus asked, puzzled. "Why should I be hurt? I lay down for just a moment. It's been a very long evening. I must have drifted off to sleep."

"Asleep!"

"Fabrizio, did you see the —" Only then did Mangus realize that the queen was also looking down at him. "My lady!" he said, and struggled to get up.

Fabrizio helped him come to his feet.

"My lady," Mangus said again, "I humbly beg your pardon . . ."

The queen gazed at Mangus suspiciously. "This is the king's private chapel," she said stiffly. "No one but the family is permitted to enter."

"My lady . . ." Mangus stammered. "With permission . . . I was in need of peace and contemplation. I . . . found my way . . . here. I humbly beg your pardon. I'm old and tire too easily. This evening's events have left me exhausted beyond measure."

"Are you speaking about the ghost?" she said.

"Yes . . . exactly . . . the ghost." Mangus pressed his gloved hands together, barely looking up at her, the very image of humility.

"I have just seen it," she said.

Mangus looked at her sheepishly. "Did you, my lady?"

"I did, your servant and I. We were standing at the place where it came to my daughter when it appeared."

"As I recall, you had not seen it before."

"No, I had not."

"And, with permission, you doubted its existence."

Fabrizio, detecting a hint of a smile about his master's lips, wondered if Mangus would dare mock the queen about ghosts as he had so often done with him.

She said, "I did doubt, but no more."

Mangus turned, cocked his head, and looked at Fabrizio. "And you, my faithful servant, did you see it?" he asked.

"Yes, Master."

"Did it look like the ghost you saw before?"

"Master, I don't understand the question."

"I presume," Mangus continued gravely but with a sparkle in his eyes, "by your understanding, there are many kinds of spirits who haunt this world of ours — tormented souls who cannot find their rest in the bosom of the Lord. I was merely asking if you saw the same vision we saw earlier this evening."

"Master, I assure you, it was exactly the same."

"Did it frighten you as much?" Mangus asked.

"It was terrible," the queen interjected. "And I can attest that it was real. I never should have doubted my daughter. Signore, you must help her by driving this ghost away. I fear it will do us all some great harm."

"There is that danger," Mangus agreed. "But I think I may be able to help her."

"Pray, do it quickly," the queen said, drawing herself up to her full height. "You will be amply rewarded."

"I will try as hard as I can," Mangus offered. "As for now . . . I must again beg pardon for my intrusion."

"No harm was done," the queen returned grandly. "But in the morning you must advise the king what to do. In matters of the supernatural, he believes in you beyond all others. Now, if you two will leave me, I should like to avail myself of prayer and contemplation."

Mangus bowed. "Of course, my lady. Fabrizio, come away." He reached out for support.

Fabrizio hastened to take his arm, and the two made their way to the door.

"With permission," Mangus murmured again, and the two stepped into the hall.

No sooner did they leave than Mangus whispered, "The door, Fabrizio, shut it!"

Fabrizio closed the door.

Mangus said, "Can you guide me back to our chamber?" His voice was neither hesitant nor halting as it had been when he was with the queen.

"Yes, Master," Fabrizio said, stealing an inquiring glance at Mangus.

They started off, the old man setting so quick a pace, Fabrizio could hardly keep up. "There," Mangus said, "you should be pleased. I did not tell the truth."

"What do you mean, Master?"

"I was only pretending to be asleep."

Fabrizio looked at Mangus quizzically.

"This visitation — this ghost," Mangus said, "the one you saw with the queen, tell me all about it."

Fabrizio groaned inwardly. "Master, I've already said, it was the same as before."

"Did it speak this time, too?"

"Not a word," Fabrizio said.

"Good," Mangus said. "I'm pleased to hear you say so."

"Pleased?" Fabrizio exclaimed, more and more puzzled. "I don't understand."

"Fabrizio," Mangus said with more than a touch of merriment in his voice, "I have solved the mystery."

Fabrizio came to a halt. "Master! What do you mean?"

"Just as I said. I know where the so-called ghost came from. I know how it appeared in that place where the princess — and you and I — observed it. More than that, I'm not yet prepared to say. Other things must still be discovered. But my reason shall uncover those, too," he added with a chuckle.

Fabrizio stared at his master with amazement. "Master, are you feeling well?"

"Perfectly fine. Why do you ask?"

"With permission, Master, you don't sound like yourself. First, you admitted you lied. Then you laughed. You almost seem like a regular person. What have you found?"

Mangus smiled. "You shall see. But I need a little more time. First, however, I wish to return to our chamber. Though happy, I am fatigued. I should have been asleep a long time ago."

"You are tired, Master."

"Mostly old," Mangus replied. "But not," he added with a grin, "so old as not to be able to outthink the young."

Fabrizio, knowing Mangus would not say another word until he chose to, guided him back to their chamber. As they went, he tried to think out what it was that Mangus had discovered. He could not.

As they came around the last corner of the corridor that led to their chamber, they found armed soldiers milling about their door.

"What is this . . . ?" Mangus murmured.

The moment one of the soldiers saw Mangus, they called into the chamber. The next moment, Count Scarazoni burst from the room. With him was Princess Teresina.

"Halt!" Scarazoni cried out.

Mangus and Fabrizio stood still.

Fabrizio stared at Teresina, trying to catch her eye. She looked away, appearing cold and aloof.

"Mangus," Count Scarazoni called out. "You have been betrayed."

"My lord, I don't understand."

"That boy of yours. Do you know who he is?"

"Fabrizio? He's my trusted servant. My apprentice."

"He's a spy," Count Scarazoni returned. "He has been discovered trying to ferret out secrets."

"Why, as for that, my lord," Mangus pleaded, "it's true I have asked him to look and listen for what might be —"

"Mangus," Scarazoni interrupted, "the boy has brazenly sought out the princess Teresina and attempted to pry state secrets from her."

"The princess!" Mangus cried with disbelief. "My lord, that's not possible."

Scarazoni spoke to the girl. "Tell the magician what you told me," he commanded.

The princess, haughty and cold, stepped forward. "This common boy attempted to win my confidence," she began. "He presumed to call himself my friend and inquired of family matters and other state secrets. I denounce him for the spy he is."

"But, Princess!" Fabrizio cried, hardly believing what he was hearing. "You know that's untrue!"

"Silence!" Count Scarazoni commanded.

"My lady," Mangus said, "with permission, Fabrizio is loyal and kind, doing only as he has been asked. . . ."

"Boy," Scarazoni barked, "do you deny that you met secretly with the princess at night and talked? Do you?"

"My lord, I only did as she —"

"Do you deny it?"

Fabrizio hung his head. "No."

Mangus gazed upon him with astonishment.

"Take the boy away," Scarazoni said to his soldiers.

"My lord," Teresina said, "one request!"

"Of course."

"Place him in the lower dungeon. The one reserved for traitors."

Scarazoni smiled. "An excellent idea, Princess. I'll do so with pleasure."

Mangus tried to intervene. "My lord, this boy —"

Brushing Mangus aside, two soldiers stepped forward, took the bewildered Fabrizio by his arms, wheeled him about, and marched him off. Too dumbfounded to make any resistance, all the boy could manage was a frightened glance back at Mangus. The old man was staring after him with great dismay.

"Turn around!" one of the soldiers barked. Fabrizio, weak-kneed, was pulled along around a bend in the corridor.

"Out of the way!" one of the soldiers cried.

Fabrizio looked up just in time to see Rinaldo. What was he doing there?

The soldiers led Fabrizio into the very lowest regions of the castello. Once there, they flung him into a dark dungeon, slammed the door shut, turned the key in the lock, and left him alone.

For a long while, Fabrizio lay where he had been thrown, hardly believing the sudden turn of events. Why had the princess turned against him? How could he have judged her so wrong, or, for that matter, she judge him so ill? He asked himself if she could have been using him for some purpose he did not understand. If so, what purpose could she have? And was it an accident that Rinaldo had suddenly appeared? Then he wondered if there was a connection between Mangus's discovery and his arrest, and if he would live long enough to know what that discovery was. He could make no sense of any of it.

"I was foolish to even think I could be the princess's friend," he chided himself. Ruefully, he recalled the old saying "You may wrap a monkey in the skin of a lion, but he remains a monkey."

Once calm, Fabrizio sat up and felt about. Though he could see nothing, he was fairly sure he was upon a flat stone floor. The stones were slimy. A foul stench filled the air.

He began to crawl about, only to bang his head against a stone wall. Turning, he crawled in a different direction. Very quickly he gained a sense of the room's size. It was square and not very large.

At one point he came upon some hard, long, and lumpish things. He felt them carefully only to realize that they were bones, human bones. It brought goose bumps to his body.

Exhausted as well as frightened, Fabrizio propped himself up against one of the cold, damp walls. He had little doubt about his own fate. It was not a question of if he were to be killed, but merely when and how it would happen. It was all too horrible to contemplate.

But Fabrizio was too tired, too numb to think with clarity. He had slept little the night before, and not much more during the day. Though fearful of what might happen to him if he closed his eyes, he kept nodding off. And he was sound asleep when a hand touched his face and called his name.

chapter 21

It was Princess Teresina. With candle in hand, a soft yellow glow illuminated her smiling face. Fabrizio gazed at her with bafflement and anger, hardly knowing what to say.

"Wasn't I wonderfully clever, Fabrizio?" she said with a laugh. "Didn't I save and protect you just as I said I would?"

"My lady," Fabrizio managed to say, "you betrayed me."

"Silly boy! You didn't believe those things I said to Count Scarazoni, did you?"

"He believed them," Fabrizio returned glumly.

"But that was exactly what I wished. Oh, Fabrizio," she pouted, "I can see you don't appreciate what I've done for you."

"My lady, in truth, I do not. You caused me to be placed in this dreadful place. Any moment now they will come to kill me."

"The name is Teresina, Fabrizio," she said as if it were she who had been insulted. "Have you forgotten our friendship so soon? But if you're so silly that you can't know what I've done, I'll be patient and explain it to you."

"My lady, when Gabriel blows his horn, even the deaf will listen."

"Fabrizio, the castello has no secrets. I was afraid Scarazoni would learn of our friendship and do you harm. By accusing you of being a spy, I knew he would put you in one of our dungeons where you would be safe from harm. And that was exactly what he did.

"As for executing you, it is a time-honored tradition — and my father the king believes deeply in traditions — that when one is condemned to die, you must suffer a week of waiting before you are executed. So you see, Fabrizio, fear not. There is time enough for you to help me."

Fabrizio gazed at her in weary disbelief.

"The important thing," she went on, "is this: By being here, you can use your magic to convince Mangus that there truly is a ghost, and that, moreover, the ghost is my murdered brother's troubled spirit. When you do that, I know I'll be kept from this marriage.

"And, Fabrizio, even as you do this, Count Scarazoni won't be able to blame you, because he'll think you're here. Don't you see," she concluded, "being here is a perfect mask for doing what I wish."

"But Scarazoni might kill me!" Fabrizio cried.

"As to that, Fabrizio," Teresina said with the utmost seriousness, "I've no doubt you can protect yourself. In any case, death is always a risk in a conspiracy. That's what makes it so thrilling. How could it be otherwise? It's not a game for the fainthearted."

"Game!" Fabrizio cried, turning from her bright and cheerful face. It was then he noticed an open trapdoor in a corner.

"Is that the way you got in here?" he asked.

Teresina laughed. "That's why I suggested this cell. It has a secret entry. Now you can come and go at will."

"You astonish me," he said.

"No less than you amaze me with your powers," she replied sweetly.

"Why was such a door even built?"

"Oh, Fabrizio, how little you understand. In matters of state it's sometimes necessary to execute a prisoner in private," she explained in a matter-of-fact fashion.

Fabrizio shuddered. "What is the hour?" he said.

"You lazy boy, you have slept almost the whole day away. It's night. Have you eaten?" she inquired.

He shook his head.

"Then you must come with me," she said, and moved toward the secret door.

"But what if they come and don't find me here?"

"That would be a wonderful thing. They don't know about this door. From inside the room, it's completely hidden. If they find you gone, they'll respect your magic even more."

Fabrizio sighed. The girl seemed to have an answer for everything. "Teresina," he asked, "have you seen my master?"

"Not since your arrest."

"I must go to him. He'll be very worried about me. He needs me to care for him."

"For a low boy, you do act nobly," she said sincerely. "Let me think — he is in the Saint Stephano chamber. . . ." She smiled. "Nothing could be easier."

She went to the trapdoor, lifted it, then let

Fabrizio drop down first. Following, she closed the door behind them. Her candlelight revealed a narrow passageway lined with crumbling stone. At the end of the passageway, a flight of spiral stone steps rose into murky darkness. Teresina handed Fabrizio the candle and urged him to lead the way.

It was a hard climb. The steps were steep and twisted. There was considerable rubble, too, which made it difficult to navigate. Cobwebs were everywhere. Once, twice, they came to narrow landings where Fabrizio observed doors set into walls. Each time they reached them, he looked around, but Teresina shook her head.

Only when they reached the third landing did she call upon him to stop. Fabrizio observed a wooden door set into the wall. Teresina squeezed past him. "Be very quiet," she warned, and put her ear against the door, listening. "I think we're safe," she whispered, and blew the candle out. From the sound of jangling, Fabrizio was certain she took a key from a pocket, turned a lock, then opened the door.

There was light beyond.

She stuck her head out. "Quickly!" she urged, and darted forward into an empty corridor. After a short dash, they came to a wall tapestry, which Teresina lifted by a corner, revealing a door. She shoved it in, and the two entered yet another passageway.

"It will be dark," she cautioned. "But it's not far."

"Where will we be then?" Fabrizio asked.

Teresina giggled. "You shall see."

It was so dark, Fabrizio could only hear Teresina move before him. Using his hands to feel his way, he came to another flight of steps.

"Almost there," the princess said from above.

Fabrizio crept along.

"Here," she finally said. He heard a bump. A door swung open. To Fabrizio's surprise, they stepped into his own chamber. The door was nothing less than the picture of the Blessed Martyr, Saint Stephano.

Mangus was on his bed, propped up against the wall. As Fabrizio came forward, he looked at the boy with amazement. "Fabrizio!" he cried. "I . . . I feared I would never see you again." Impulsively he got up and embraced the boy warmly. Fabrizio hugged him back.

Then, when Mangus realized Princess Teresina was with him, he made something of a bow. "But where did . . . you come from?" Mangus stammered. "I was told you had been put in the dungeon."

"The princess came for me," Fabrizio explained. "She knows all the hidden passageways in the castello and can go everywhere she wants and never be seen. It was she who came to free me."

"I'm afraid I don't understand," Mangus said. "With permission, my lady, I thought you denounced the boy as a traitor."

"You two are so silly!" Teresina exclaimed. "As I told Fabrizio, it was merely a trick to put him out of harm's way. If one is to hold power," she said with the utmost seriousness, "as I intend to, one must master the skills of deception."

"With permission, my lady," Mangus said, "I must sit."

"We are all friends here," she said.

"Are we?" Mangus asked. "I'm pleased to hear it. But that passageway — through which you just arrived — is it known by many?"

"I don't think so," she replied. "My brother, perhaps."

"Ah! Your brother. How he haunts us."

"Ah! Do you then believe the ghost is he?" she exclaimed.

Mangus held up his hands. "Please, with permission," he said, "you said we are friends. My lady, I must first understand how you and my assistant have become such companions."

"Remember, Master," Fabrizio said in embarrassed haste, "two nights ago, you asked me to fetch water. When I went about the castello, I became lost. I met the princess then."

"We saw the ghost," Teresina said with some pride. "Together."

"Did you?" Mangus said, eyeing Fabrizio critically. "You never told me."

"I swore him to secrecy," the princess said.

"And have you met again?" Mangus asked.

"Only twice," Fabrizio said. "In the princess's private chambers, and then again after the ghost came — that time when you were there and the ghost spoke."

"I see," Mangus said, and rubbed his hands.

"Forgive me, Master," Fabrizio said.

"I ordered him to be secretive," Teresina said. "As Fabrizio informed me, you, in your dwindling years, have renounced all your potent magic powers. Out of fatherly love you have passed these powers to Fabrizio so that he may do great wonders. I'm sure that's why the ghost called upon him."

Mangus made a wry face. "Was that the way Fabrizio explained it?"

"Master . . ." the boy started to protest. But before he could say more, Teresina went on.

"Magician — if I may call you so — it does not matter what Fabrizio said or did not say. It is a fine and noble truth that does you much honor. Most importantly, it was what I wished."

"I see," Mangus mumbled. He looked up and winked at Fabrizio, something the boy had never seen him do before.

"You see," Teresina went on, "I commanded him to convince you, with all his powers, that the ghost is real."

"Will he do so now?"

"He has promised, and Fabrizio keeps his promises."

"But if I have no powers, what good am I to you?" Mangus asked.

"My father, the king, believes in you. Though Fabrizio turned lead to gold, he still wouldn't listen to such a low one."

"As for the ghost," Mangus said, and folded his arms over his chest in an attitude of defiance, "there is none."

"But did you not see it for yourself?" Teresina demanded.

"What I saw," he continued, "though it looked like a ghost, was nothing more than a hoax."

"My brother's ghost, a hoax?" Teresina said with anger.

"Master," Fabrizio said, "just before I was taken away, you said you had solved the mystery. Can you explain?"

"I can," he returned.

"But will you?" Fabrizio pleaded.

Instead of answering, Mangus turned to the Princess. "Princess," he said, "when you and I spoke, you said you freely accepted this marriage to Scarazoni. Is that true?"

"No," she admitted.

"Very well. I believe you now. I have one further question." He looked at her squarely and said, "Do you have proof your brother died?"

"The ghost . . . ," the princess said. "That is the proof."

Mangus shook his head.

"Master," Fabrizio added, "I saw it three times!"

"Would you like to see it a fourth time?" Mangus asked.

"I never want to see it again," Fabrizio assured him.

"And you, Princess? Did you wish to see it?"

Teresina became serious. "The ghost comes on his own."

"Does it?"

"Of course," she said quietly.

"Princess, with permission, do you know a way to your family chapel so that we may get there without being seen?"

Teresina gazed hard at Mangus. He stared back. It was as if they were having a duel without words.

"Yes," she said.

"Then, with permission, lead us."

"Master," Fabrizio said, "what has this to do with the ghost?"

"Ah, Fabrizio, whereas I do not believe in ghosts, I do believe in ghost stories. And, as in a story, I can only answer your question by saying, 'When we are at the chapel, all shall be revealed.'"

chapter 22

Teresina led the way to the chapel by a number of hidden passages as well as some swift darting — as much as Mangus could dart — along empty corridors.

She was unusually quiet and pensive. By contrast, Mangus had an almost jovial air, as if he were enjoying himself. Fabrizio was puzzled.

They entered the chapel by the main door. It was, as before, dim. The altar flame burned low. A few puny, bent tapers glowed faithfully. The smell of incense was strong. It being night, no light came through the stained-glass window on the outside wall, though a faint incandescence did come through the inside wall of green glass.

Mangus knelt before the altar and crossed himself. Teresina and Fabrizio did the same. Then the magician rose.

"My lady," Mangus said to Teresina in a hushed voice, "I think it would be wise if we were undisturbed. Can the door be locked from the inside?"

Though there was hesitation in Teresina's manner, she said, "Yes," and did so.

"Good," Mangus said. "Now we should be secure."

Recalling the secret cabinet door through which he had entered before with Rinaldo, Fabrizio blurted out, "Master, there is another door."

Mangus swung about. "Is there?"

Fabrizio nodded.

"How did you come to know of this? From the princess?"

"Yes, it was me," she said quickly. Too quickly.

Mangus noted her fast intervention. "My lady, with permission, my question was addressed to my powerful servant." He looked at Fabrizio again. "Give me *your* answer, Fabrizio," he said.

"It was the kitchen boy," Fabrizio said.

"Magician . . . ," Teresina started to say with impatience only to have Mangus go on to say, "Was that, Fabrizio, by some chance, the one who brought us food yesterday?"

Fabrizio nodded. "And it was he who led me to the chapel that time I overheard Scarazoni and Addetto talking."

"And was he the same one who had the missing statue of Our Lady, given him, so he claimed, by the queen?"

"Yes, Master."

"I see. And how does such a low one come to know of this secret way?"

"He said it was a servants' entrance," Fabrizio replied.

"Where is this entryway?" Mangus inquired.

"Within that closet." Fabrizio pointed across the room. "It leads to a corridor."

Mangus looked at the princess for affirmation. "Is he right?" he asked.

"Yes."

"And can this second door be secured? With permission, we need to be alone."

The princess glanced at Fabrizio — none too happily, he thought. "Yes," she said.

"Fabrizio," Mangus said, "please do so."

Once Fabrizio had latched the closet door, Mangus turned to the princess. "Now then," he began, "as to the matter of the so-called ghost. My lady, with permission, will you be kind enough to give me brief responses to my questions?"

"Maybe," she said. Her face was drawn, her hands clenched in fists.

"If I understand the design of the castello, this chapel is on a level higher than the corridor where your own chambers are situated, is that correct?"

"Yes."

"The chapel is, moreover, placed between two walls. One wall looks out to the blessed heavens." He gestured toward the stained glass.

"Yes."

"And," Mangus continued, turning slightly, "there is this inner wall that allows some light to enter from a corridor. Yes?"

"Yes."

"That corridor below is where we can find the niche, where your apparition appeared. Am I understanding this properly, my lady?" he prompted anew.

"Yes."

"Fabrizio," he said, "go against the inner windows. Look down through them."

Though Fabrizio sensed that Mangus was toying with him, he did as he was told.

"What do you see?" Mangus requested.

"A corridor," he said.

"Princess, am I right to say that this is the corridor where your chambers are to be found?"

"Yes."

"Excellent. I can assure you if you stand where you are, you may hear everything said from there. Now, then, Fabrizio, my magical boy, take up a lighted taper."

Puzzled, Fabrizio did so.

"Use that taper to light that candle . . . *there!*" Mangus pointed toward the tall candelabra with the one fat candle. Directly behind the candle socket was the convex silver plate, designed, as Fabrizio had noticed before, to reflect candlelight back into the room. The whole apparatus was not much bigger than he was.

"Go on," Mangus insisted, "light the candle."

Fabrizio did so.

As soon as he did, the chapel grew brighter by virtue of the reflective plate.

"Now, Fabrizio," Mangus continued, "go behind that candle. You will see that the reflecting plate is on a bracket that moves. By such means it can direct light in one direction or another. See if I am correct."

It was as Mangus said. The reflecting plate was mounted on an L-shaped bracket, which in turn looped around the stem of the candleholder, allowing it to move around.

"Is it all as I have said?" he asked.

"Yes, Master."

"Now, then, move the reflecting plate about."

When Fabrizio did as told, a spot of blurry light moved around the chapel.

"Excellent. Now, Fabrizio, with care, bring the candelabra over there." He pointed to the windows in the inner wall.

Fabrizio glanced at the princess. She was stony faced. More than once he sensed that she was about to speak, though she held back. He did what his master asked.

"Very good," Mangus said. "Now, do you see that long box below that inner window?"

"Yes, Master."

"Go to it. Note, if you will, the drops of wax upon it. They are only at one end. Move the box so that one narrow end is butted against the wall by the inner windows. The other end — with the wax drippings — should extend into the room. Good. Now lift this candelabra and place it upon the box. Over the drippings. Well done. In some respects, Fabrizio, you follow orders well.

"Princess," Mangus went on, "with permission, please stand upon the box — opposite the candleholder — close to the windows."

She hesitated.

"Princess, I merely wish to show you your ghost."

Frowning, Teresina stood where Mangus bid her, little more than an arm's length from the large candle.

"Now, Fabrizio, using the reflecting plate, make sure the light beam made by the candle is aimed right at the princess, and is, moreover, tilted up. Of course, some wax may drip upon the box. No matter. It has done so before."

Fabrizio did as he was instructed.

"Now, Princess, be so good as to move your arms. And you, Fabrizio, as she does, look out the window — being careful not to block the beam of reflected candlelight. Observe the corridor below. What do you see?"

Fabrizio looked. At first he did not know what it was he was supposed to see. Then, to his astonishment, he grasped it: Upon the wall below was a bright *green* glow. And since the princess stood before the reflected candlelight, a shadowy, human form was projected there.

"What do you see?" Mangus asked with something like glee.

To which an awestruck Fabrizio answered, "The ghost."

"Bravo, Fabrizio! The light from the candle is reflected through the glass. The glass, being green, turns that light into a greenish hue. The reflected green light falls below — upon the wall. With practice, it can be aimed right into the niche. It thereby gives the impression that a form is *in* the niche. Recall the last time you saw the ghost, Fabrizio. It was I who made it.

"Princess," Mangus continued, "if you will be good enough to exchange places with Fabrizio, you may see all that he has seen."

"It is not necessary," she replied stiffly.

Mangus, smiling, said, "And why not?"

"I have seen it before."

"Indeed? Have you? Very well, Princess, is this not your ghost?"

Fabrizio turned to Teresina. She was very angry. Mangus, unperturbed, was returning her gaze steadily, a smile upon his lips.

She refused to answer his question.

"But, Master," Fabrizio cried, "are you saying that it was the princess who made this vision?"

"I am."

"But how can that be?"

"You have seen it for yourself."

"Master," Fabrizio said boldly, "you do not understand me. I stood by the princess when she saw the ghost. How could she have been here and there at the same time?"

"Well reasoned, Fabrizio. You are correct. She could not be in two places at once. Therefore, she had to be working with an accomplice. With permission, my lady, would you care to inform us who that person is?"

"No," she said.

"Do you wish me to guess?"

"No."

"Princess," Mangus continued evenly, "you — and your unknown friend — agreed upon the ghost's appearance. No, no, do not speak. Not yet. You hoped to convince your father — who is very superstitious — that you are haunted. That would keep you from the marriage that Count Scarazoni so much desires. Then Count Scarazoni asked me to come here. He knows I am not a wizard and that I don't believe in ghosts. But your father believes otherwise. The count thinks, what better person to inform your father that you are not haunted? You think otherwise. You hoped I would say there *is* a ghost. Am I correct in all of this?"

Teresina made no reply.

"However," Mangus continued, "when I came, you heard me say I don't believe in ghosts, so you turned to Fabrizio to support your claim. By convincing him there was a ghost, you hoped he would convince me."

Still, Teresina said nothing.

"Of course," Mangus continued gently, "you have had a bigger design. You wish to bring down Count Scarazoni. You wish to accuse him of the murder of your brother, the prince. You wish to enlist Fabrizio here in your plot. You believe he can do magic. Therefore, you had the ghost speak to him. Have I seen it all?"

"Except you," she finally said bitterly, "have only helped Count Scarazoni."

"My lady," Mangus replied with great gravity, "I was brought here to tell the truth."

"You do not understand," she said severely.

"But I think I do."

"How can you?"

"Because I believe I can name your accomplice, too."

Teresina drew herself up. "It would take magic — which you say you do not have — to know," she returned scornfully.

"Not magic, my lady, reason."

"Who, then?" she challenged.

But before Mangus could speak, there came a rapping from within the cabinet door. "Teresina! Let me in. Are you in danger?"

Mangus laughed. "What was it that the king said when we first learned of this matter? He said, 'In the middle of the night, she' — meaning you, my lady — 'goes to the chapel and seeks guidance.' Now we are about to know from whom that guidance comes."

The voice called again. "Let me in! Teresina, can you hear me? It's our meeting time."

A look of puzzlement came to Mangus's face. "Princess," he said softly, "do you recognize this voice?"

"Yes."

"But I thought . . ." Mangus did not complete the sentence. Instead, he said, "My lady, do you wish Fabrizio to open the cabinet door or not?"

Teresina remained perfectly still — as if not

sure what to do. Then, rather brusquely, she said, "He may open the door."

Mangus said, "Let us see this accomplice. Fabrizio, please . . ."

Fabrizio went to the cabinet and released the latch on the door. Not knowing what to expect, he stepped back. Gradually, the door opened. Upon the threshold stood Queen Jovanna.

chapter 23

From the expression on her face, the queen was as surprised to see Mangus and Fabrizio as they were to see her.

With a questioning look, she turned from Teresina to Mangus, to Fabrizio, then to Teresina again. "Did you bring him here?" the queen finally asked her daughter.

"There was no choice, Mother," she said softly. "He knows all."

The queen looked haughtily at Mangus, then around the chapel, her gaze coming to rest upon the large candelabra that still sat upon the box. "How did he discover it?" the queen demanded.

"I don't know," Teresina said, quite dispirited.

"With permission, my lady," Mangus said with a slight bow of his head. "It was reason that led me here. If one believes — as I do — that there are no such things as ghosts, the task becomes simple. I needed to search for the way by which a vague, green light could be made to appear upon a wall."

"Traitor!" the queen hissed at him.

Mangus, refusing to be ruffled, only bowed again, as if to applause. Whatever momentary confusion he had experienced when the queen entered the chapel was gone. He was enjoying himself.

"My lady," he said soothingly, "with permission, though I believe I have a fair understanding of what transpired here, perhaps it is you who can best explain the circumstances. It will complete my grasp of what has occurred."

Fabrizio saw the queen and princess exchange another look. Whatever communication passed between them, it was enough to cause the queen to speak.

"It began," the queen started, "because a great enmity existed between my son and Scarazoni. Prince Lorenzo felt Scarazoni had far too much influence upon his father. The king, who is not strong willed and is very superstitious, tried to smooth things over.

"Some three months ago, Scarazoni asked the prince to deliver a personal message to the pope in Rome and so be blessed as well.

"The prince could not, would not, be opposed to such an expedition. He had little reason to object. He was of age. It seemed reasonable. In any case, the king was easily swayed by Scarazoni and agreed that the prince should go.

"In short order, a bodyguard — chosen by Count Scarazoni — was selected to go with the prince. Off they went.

"For a while we heard nothing. Then came the shocking news that the prince had been killed on the road. Not only had his body vanished, his bodyguard had disappeared. But as proof of my son's death, we were sent — along with the news — his bloody garments, complete with knife holes. I have them yet.

"When I heard the news, I had little doubt that Scarazoni was behind it all. But the count, feigning innocence in this matter, insisted that the prince might still be found alive and a request for ransom would come. After all, without the body there was no proof the prince had died. He even sent out search parties to look for him.

"Moreover, he argued that the news should remain a secret from the public. The heir to the kingdom — murdered! If the news had spread, it would cause unrest. In matters of state, unrest and uncertainty breed disruption.

"The king, frightened, agreed. Then Count Scarazoni, acting swiftly, convinced my husband he should marry Teresina, claiming the alliance would strengthen the kingdom. All would be done in secrecy and great haste.

"My husband, the king, consulted his astrological charts and determined that the marriage could only take place on a certain date — two days hence.

"One night, while my daughter and I were in this chapel trying to decide what to do, the great candle was lit. We saw the possibility of creating the ghost by using the reflected light. We hoped to achieve two things: to hold off the marriage and, by saying the ghost was my son's, to keep Scarazoni in check."

"What made you choose that particular niche?" Mangus asked.

The queen said, "It was the easiest to illuminate."

Fabrizio recalled how the queen had admitted removing the statue of Our Blessed Lady.

The queen continued. "At first our plan worked. The king became very nervous about the so-called haunting. But Count Scarazoni is no fool. He grew suspicious. He doubted the existence of the ghost. We dared not show the ghost to him, fearful he would see how it was done. If he did, all might be lost. As for me, to say I saw it might cause the count to sense a plot.

"Then Scarazoni invited you here. Teresina remembered you and your trial. She believed my husband would believe you. It is as you said: If you agreed there was a ghost, he would have accepted it. The wedding would not take place."

Mangus smiled. "But when you learned I did not believe in ghosts, you turned to Fabrizio. No doubt the boy did tricks to suggest he had magical powers. You encouraged him to puff him up in hopes he would convince me."

Fabrizio felt very much the fool.

Then the queen said to Mangus, "I still find it difficult to believe you do not possess some kind of magic."

"And why is that, my lady?"

"You barely ventured from your chamber, yet you have discovered all."

"I could not have done what I have done without Fabrizio. Even so, I freely confess, it was not you I expected, Queen."

"Who, then?"

"It does not matter."

"With permission, Queen," Fabrizio suddenly said, "might I ask a question?"

"You may," she said.

"Was that you listening outside the princess's door when she and I made plans?"

"It was," the queen said. "It enabled me to know that you and the magician would look for the ghost that night — which was exactly what we wanted. But when you came after me, I left a token to confuse you. Count Scarazoni's glove."

"And the death of Signore Addetto?"

"Scarazoni, I suppose. But now that you know what's happened," the queen said to Mangus, "what do you intend to do?"

Mangus, growing serious, bowed his head and rubbed his hands. His silence was long. When he looked up, he made a humble bow. "My ladies, with permission, I must first congratulate you for having made this clever scheme. As one who has, in his time, concocted much false mystery, I can attest to it being well thought out and executed.

"However, I was brought here by the king to

rid the castello of the ghost. There is nothing more for me to do than to inform him of what I know."

"Then you will do my daughter and Pergamontio a great disservice," the queen said angrily. "You will deliver Teresina into a disgraceful and deceitful marriage. It will only be a matter of time before Count Scarazoni becomes the king. My son's murder will go unavenged."

"That may well be," Mangus said sadly. "But there is my desire to tell the truth."

"Then all is lost," the princess said, and she turned toward the door.

Fabrizio called out, "My ladies, Master, with permission, I have an idea about what to do."

All three turned to him with surprise.

"If I understand all that's been said, what needs to be done is to find a way to convince the king that Count Scarazoni has deceived him."

"He will never believe it," the queen interjected angrily. "I've tried to tell him many times. He refuses to listen."

"But, with permission," Fabrizio went on, "what if we could get the *ghost* to inform him of Scarazoni's treachery? Might not that work?"

"Fabrizio!" Mangus cried. "How can you still believe in such a thing?"

"No, no, Master, you misunderstand me. All have said the king is a great believer in ghosts. Is that not true, my lady?"

"It is," the queen said.

"And I overheard Count Scarazoni say *he* doesn't believe in them."

"That's so," agreed the princess.

"But, then," Fabrizio said, "you know what they say, 'Men don't believe in shovels until called upon to dig.'"

"Fabrizio," Mangus cried, "no nonsense!"

"With permission, why not use the ghost to tell the truth? Master, you wish to speak the truth and are a great illusionist. My lady, you wish to speak the truth and expose Count Scarazoni for the murderer that he is. Princess, you wish to speak the truth and you love excitement. Bring the ghost before the king and get it to speak the truth. Perhaps the king will believe."

It was Teresina who said, "How could we do it?"

"My lady, let my master inform the king he has discovered a way to free you of the ghost forever," Fabrizio explained. "Let him further say that to do so he must bring this ghost forward so that it may speak of its troubled sleep.

"The king will surely agree to such a notion. And how could Scarazoni say no? Then, Master, we'll do what we've done so well before, create the *illusion* of magic. Like our performances of old with smoke and light, the ghost shall appear. That will be because I'll be here, using the candle. Then I'll make the ghost speak and denounce Count Scarazoni."

"Can all that be done?" the queen asked in amazement.

"My lady," Fabrizio said, "I assure you, Mangus the Magician is an illusionist of great skill. He can create wonderful effects. They will fool anyone. I've seen him do so — before his trial."

Teresina clapped her hands. "Oh, Fabrizio, you are the most brilliant of us all! Didn't I say you would be the one to save us! It will work. I know it will."

The queen agreed just as readily. "If it could happen just as the boy suggests, it would be a fine thing."

But Mangus shook his head. "Fabrizio," he said with severity, "you know I've foresworn all such so-called magical performances. You know what great harm and distress they have caused. They delude people. They make them think there is really magic. It's wrong, and I will not do it."

"But, Master," Fabrizio cried, "it would do great good!"

"Fabrizio," Mangus replied severely, "can something good come from something so wrong?"

"With permission, Master," Fabrizio said boldly, "if the princess is saved from the marriage and the king is kept safe from treason and worse by our revealing the plots of Count Scarazoni, would not all that be good?"

"It would," Mangus acknowledged grudgingly.

"And, Master, I beg you to note that, above all, our ghost will only speak the truth."

Mangus grew thoughtful. "What if Count Scarazoni sees through it? He will be provoked to great wrath. If we fail, our lives will be instantly forfeited."

"But, Signore," the queen said, "if we do nothing, the results could be worse."

Mangus rubbed his hands.

"Master," Fabrizio pressed, "you said you did not believe in ghosts, only in ghost stories. But can't a story speak the truth? You know what they say, 'Artists tell lies to tell the truth.' And you, master, are a great artist."

Mangus shook his head and laughed. "Fabrizio," he said, "you have the most profound mix of ignorance and cleverness I've ever known."

"Will you do it, then?" asked Teresina.

The old magician sighed, looked around, and said, "If you will all help me, yes."

It was quickly agreed that the princess would be at the very center of the scheme. She would carry messages from each to the others. This pleased her greatly. Whereas before she had been cast down, she was once again full of energy.

Their plan made, Princess Teresina led Mangus back to his chamber and Fabrizio to his dungeon cell. The queen went to her rooms by herself.

As Fabrizio lay down in the darkness, he thought of all he had learned. But as he tried to reason it out, there was something that did not seem right to him, something yet incomplete. Over and over he examined it, trying to ferret out the bother in his brain. When he visualized the image of the princess standing before the candelabra, it did not seem right. Or was it that Mangus was surprised when the queen entered the chapel? It did not all make complete sense.

But he was too fatigued to go beyond his own perplexity. Instead, he fell asleep.

In another part of the castello, the princess and the queen had a quick and private meeting.

"Mother," whispered Teresina with great excitement, "the magician thinks he understands it all."

"We'll not tell him otherwise," the queen cautioned. "But have no doubt, Teresina, we're playing a most dangerous game."

Teresina shivered with delight. "It makes me . . . hungry."

"Well, then," the queen said, "inform the kitchen."

"Oh, Mother," Teresina said, squeezing her hands together with excitement, "I do love conspiracies!"

chapter 24

In the morning it fell to Mangus to begin the great intrigue. As soon as the castello was astir, he sent a message to the king and requested an urgent audience. It was granted promptly.

He met with the king in a private room. Count Scarazoni as well as the queen were in attendance. The king was in a state of extreme anxiety. His clothing was disheveled, his eyes bloodshot, his hands in constant movement. From time to time he chewed upon the side of his thumb.

The queen, by his side, was much more composed. She fixed her eyes on Mangus and never once shifted them away.

Count Scarazoni was in a froth of anger. There was, moreover, a pallor to his face that suggested great worry. His eyes kept shifting nervously between Mangus and the king.

"My lady, my lords," Mangus began with a bow, "with permission, the events of last night have allowed me to come to a much better understanding of this strange matter."

"Mangus," the count demanded, "is the ghost real? That is all the king wishes to know. Is there a ghost in this castello?"

"My lord," Mangus returned, "my understanding of these complex matters suggests that the question is not so simple."

"But, Mangus," the king cried, "if my daughter is truly haunted . . ." He covered his eyes with his hands.

"My lord," Mangus said, "with permission, there can be many kinds of haunting. A person can be haunted by a dream, a vision, a fear. A person can be haunted by an act committed, and, curiously enough, an act not done."

"Mangus," Count Scarazoni said sharply, "you prattle. Answer the king's question. Is the princess being haunted by a ghost or not?"

"My lord," Mangus returned, "my motive for having come before you is to say that I am quite certain that I can free the princess from her visions."

The count could barely suppress a triumphant smile. "Are you sure?" he asked.

"I am."

"How so?"

"My lord," Mangus began, "my skills are such that I have ways of bringing a ghost forward, making it reveal its anguish, and by so doing, banish it forever."

"How would you manage it?" It was the queen who spoke.

"My lady, it requires great care, preparation, even special instruments. But with such devices as I possess, I can call up this *thing* and make it do as I desire."

"And once you have brought this evil forward, how can you trust it?" the king demanded. "Or contain it?"

"My lord, with permission," Mangus continued softly, "it is my skill as a magician that will control it. In so doing, I, in all humility, believe I can help the princess be free from torment."

Scarazoni said, "Can you promise the haunting will — thence forward — be done with forever?"

"Yes, my lord. I can give you my word as to that."

"Then do it!"

"Mangus," the king asked nervously, "how soon after it be done?"

"This evening, I should think. If . . ."

"If what?"

"If I can have assistance."

It was the count who said, "You will have all you need."

"My lords, with permission," Mangus went on, "what I do needs to take place in the same spot and at the same time — midnight — where this thing appeared previously. May I further request that all of you — and the princess — be there."

"Done," the count said. "Anything else?" he asked.

"My lords, the apparatus I need is locked up in my home. With permission, my servant, if he could be released from his confinement, could fetch it."

"Your boy?" the king said with a blank look. "Why has he been imprisoned?"

"The princess accused him of being a traitor," Scarazoni said. "He is in a dungeon awaiting execution."

"My lord," Mangus replied evenly, "All I ask for myself is that, if I am successful, the boy's life be spared. He is, in his way, a rascal, but he is no traitor. For now, release him, let me speak to him, allow him to gather up such things as I might need from my home. Afterward, you may return him to his confinement until this exercise is over."

"There can be no deception from him," Scarazoni warned.

"My life upon it," Mangus returned humbly, "the boy shall do only as I tell him to."

No one spoke.

Then Count Scarazoni said, "I am in favor."

The king drummed nervously upon the arms of his chair with his fingers.

"My lord," the queen suddenly said, "I believe it is the thing to do. Allow the magician to make this ghost appear before us. Let it speak the truth. I'm not afraid to hear it."

The king seemed to shrink upon his chair. He put his hands over his eyes. "Yes, let it come," he whispered. "I will have my daughter free of this. I don't care what happens! Yes, Mangus, you have my permission. Raise up the ghost!"

chapter 25

Two guards — one armed, the other carrying a torch — flung open the main door of Fabrizio's cell. "Food!" one of them called.

A sleepy Fabrizio sat up, pushed the hair out of his eyes, and yawned.

The guards entered the room and stood by the door. They were immediately followed by Rinaldo. The kitchen boy was looking more bedraggled than ever. But in his hands he held half a loaf of bread and a jar of water. He placed them close to Fabrizio.

Fabrizio eyed him suspiciously. Surely, the boy was a spy, and yet it was he, Fabrizio, who was in a dungeon.

"Have no fear," Rinaldo murmured under his breath. "You will be successful."

Fabrizio stared angrily after him as he withdrew. The guards followed, locking the door behind them.

As Fabrizio drank the water and chewed on the bread, he wished he knew what was happening. As far as he was concerned, Rinaldo's words were hardly a comfort. It made him wonder — as he had done so many other times — how many others in the castello knew of what they were doing. If Count Scarazoni caught any wind of it . . .

Fabrizio had barely finished his breakfast when Teresina entered the dungeon by way of the secret trapdoor. "I have good news," she announced as she popped up. "You'll be free to go to the magician's home to get some things he needs for tonight."

"Will I be returned here?" Fabrizio asked glumly.

"I hope so. It will be so much better for us all if you are."

"I don't understand."

"Don't you see, though you will be in the chapel making the ghost, Scarazoni will believe you're here. It will make everything that much more mysterious."

"Teresina," Fabrizio whispered. "A kitchen boy was here. He hinted he knew that something was happening."

The princess made a face. "Fabrizio, are you going to worry about what some low, dirty boy says to you? Or are you going to pay heed to me?"

"To you, my lady."

"I trust so," she said, and left the way she had come.

Not long after she left, soldiers came and marched Fabrizio to where Mangus was waiting in his room. The two greeted each other warmly.

Crouching as far from the painting of Saint Stephano as possible and speaking in whispers — lest anyone be listening — Mangus told Fabrizio that he had received permission to send him back home so that he might bring back magical equipment for that night's events. He listed everything he needed. Then Mangus asked the boy to bestow loving greetings on his wife, Sophia, which Fabrizio assured his master he would do.

Five soldiers marched Fabrizio out of Castello

Pergamontio into a bright, hot day. After the dungeon gloom the blazing sun of summer almost blinded him while the heat took him by surprise. Not that he had much time to spend outside. He was quickly shoved into a hot coach with sealed windows. Then they went clattering down the hill into the lower city.

The carriage did not stop until it reached Mangus's house.

After making his way to the study, Fabrizio busied himself in the chests of magical equipment. Though he would have preferred to be alone with Sophia, one of the soldiers stayed with him all the while.

As Fabrizio gathered the necessary things, Sophia hovered near, and they managed a whispered conversation.

"My master bid me bring you his love and respect," he said. "All should go well with him. But I can't speak more."

"You will bring him my love," she returned.

"I will, Signora."

When a wicker basket was full of all that Mangus had requested, Sophia helped Fabrizio carry it to the door. Once there, it was loaded into the carriage.

"Fabrizio," Sophia said just before he climbed

back in the cab, "do you think your master will be home soon?"

"The king will be fair," Fabrizio said in a voice loud enough so the soldiers would hear.

Within the hour, Mangus had everything he needed. The area near the niche where Teresina's ghost had appeared was roped off. Soldiers were posted on guard so that none might interfere. Then Mangus and Fabrizio set about to work in earnest.

Directly in front of the niche, a little brazier was placed in which coals could safely burn. Nearby, candles were set up ready to be lit. In a semicircle before the niche, a ring of jars containing thick, musky incense was set down. There were also bowls of special powders which, when set aflame, would produce billowing smoke of different colors.

"We need as much smoke as possible, Fabrizio," Mangus explained.

"I know, Master. It's what you used to say, 'The more there is to see, the less one sees.'"

Mangus smiled.

Candles with special fuses were set about. When lit, some would sparkle. Others, which contained pockets of gunpowder, would make random, explosive sounds.

Three jars were placed near where Mangus would be standing. When their oily contents were set aflame, they would burn quickly, producing a wind that would blow through reedlike instruments, creating a soft, moaning sound.

Flags and streamers were put in place. Multicolored, each one was covered with magical signs that Mangus himself had fabricated.

Fabrizio had brought back Mangus's magician costume. It was a long green robe covered with fantastical signs, plus a three-peaked hat. From each peak a black star — cut from cloth — dangled.

Before this stage — as Mangus called it — chairs had been set down for those who would be the audience.

When all was in place, Mangus reviewed the plan in a whisper.

"As to getting out of the cell so you can create the ghost, Princess Teresina has promised to show you the necessary secret passageways. They will enable you to get to the chapel without being observed. You need to arrive shortly before midnight.

"But mind, Fabrizio," Mangus went on, "if you get to the chapel too late, the effect will not take place, and disaster will be the result. But don't get there too early, either. There's too much danger of discovery. Then, too, all might be lost."

Fabrizio assured Mangus he understood it all.

"Finally," Mangus continued, "when, in the midst of that smoke and flame, I call out, *Come to us, spirit! Show us your being! Now!* that will be your cue to make the ghost appear."

"I understand, Master."

"Excellent. Now, Fabrizio," Mangus cautioned somberly, "in this whole enterprise a very great deal depends on you. The future of all Pergamontio — not to mention our own lives — lies with you and how well you perform."

"Master," Fabrizio returned, "I promise I won't fail."

With all in readiness, there was nothing to do but wait until midnight. Mangus returned to his room while Fabrizio was escorted back to his dungeon cell.

Shortly after Fabrizio arrived, the princess appeared.

"My father is in a highly nervous state," she informed him with excitement. "He's ready to believe anything he shall see."

"And Scarazoni?"

"Oh, Fabrizio, it's altogether wonderful. He's

pacing about, a stew of wrath and tension. His hand is on his sword. He's being hard on the soldiers. You see, it makes him wild not to be in control. There's no telling what he might do.

"Here," she said, handing Fabrizio a large candle that was striped, top to bottom. "This candle tells the hours," she explained. "When the flame burns down to here" — she pointed to the second stripe from the bottom — "it will be the right time for you to come to the chapel. And then you can use it to guide you there."

Fabrizio set the candle carefully on the floor.

Then, with another lit candle in hand, Teresina showed Fabrizio the way to the chapel through a variety of back ways and secret passages. Difficult turns were repeated, and dark corners examined. Fabrizio was soon able to assure the princess he had mastered it all.

Returning to his cell, they talked only a little more.

"Oh, Fabrizio," Teresina said, "what a fine thing this shall be. Only tell me, when Mangus does these performances, do *real* spirits ever come?"

"Teresina," Fabrizio assured her, "you know I believe in ghosts. But Mangus is so skillful that though all is false, everything looks truly wondrous. He plays upon an audience as if it were a lute."

Teresina laughed with excitement, bid Fabrizio a warm good-bye, then gave him a final reminder that he must not fall asleep and miss the midnight hour. With that, she hastened from his dreary place.

Left alone, there was nothing for Fabrizio to do but wait for midnight. Though in a state of great excitement about the coming event, the more he thought about it, the more worried he became. He worried that he might even fail to find the chapel at all. What if he neglected to project the light correctly? Or what if he did not answer Mangus's questions in the proper way? Then, too, there was the possibility that he would not be loud or speak clearly enough.

Most of all, Fabrizio fretted that he would drift into sleep and miss the moment entirely. It was necessary — he told himself again and again — that he stay awake. He moved closer to the burning time candle, the better to track the hours.

But, considering all that had occurred the night before, which included having very little rest, it was hardly a wonder that — despite great struggles — he nodded, he blinked, he fell asleep.

As he slept he rolled over, knocking over the timing candle, plunging the dungeon into utter darkness.

chapter 26

Confused by the complete darkness, Fabrizio woke slowly.

With a start, he suddenly grasped the fact that the timing candle was no longer burning. Greatly alarmed, he groped for it, found it, and guessed what had happened. With a sickening sense of dread, he realized what it meant: There was no way for him to know whether he had dozed for a moment or had slept for hours. If it had been only moments, he need not worry. But if he had slept longer, was it before or after midnight?

Horrified that there was absolutely no way of answering the question, yet knowing how much depended upon him, Fabrizio fell into a state of great anxiety. One second, he was certain his sleep has lasted moments. The next, he was just as convinced he had slumbered for hours and that all was lost. Within moments of waking, he convinced himself that he must go to the chapel right away — if only to determine the time.

Feeling his way to Teresina's secret door, Fabrizio pried it up, then dropped down into the passageway. No sooner had he done that than he faced still another problem: Losing the timing candlelight meant he had lost the means to illuminate his way. When he had practiced before — with Teresina's guidance — there had been a candle in his hand. How would he ever find his way? Yet he was more convinced than ever that he must not stay in the dungeon.

Using his feet as well as his hands to feel his way, Fabrizio moved into the narrow passageway. At first there was no difficulty. There was only one way to go, and that was forward. After stumbling along for a few paces, he began to go up a winding, spiral staircase of stone.

Unfortunately, the circular motion made Fabrizio dizzy. The complete darkness made it worse. Though Fabrizio tried to go fast, he was forced to get on hands and knees and crawl.

Using his hands — like an insect's antenna —

to find his way and attempting — despite the whirling sensation in his head — to remember what level was the proper place for him to exit, he made his way up and around. Even so, he was constantly slipping, stumbling, barking his shins.

When he had gone up four levels — or was it three? — Fabrizio decided it was the *second* level he was meant to exit. Down he went only to miss the door entirely — or so he imagined was the case — which made him scamper frantically up again. By that time he was in such a state of bewilderment that he was convinced he was not just lost but late, ruining everything.

Fabrizio made up his mind that he must get off the steps and into some light — any light. With any luck he would recognize where he was. As soon as he reached a landing where he could feel a door, he pushed it open.

It took but one glance to tell him he had come to a place he had never been before. That left him with the choice of returning to the dark, spiral stairs or making an attempt at finding his way through the dimly lighted but open corridors. Desperate for light, Fabrizio made his decision quickly. He stepped into the corridor.

For a moment he remained motionless. The castello was still. That in itself alarmed Fabrizio.

Then he spied a window and, looking out, saw that it was night. Exactly how late at night it was he had no idea. All he knew was that it had been daylight when he had last entered his cell. And that meant there could be no doubt but he had slept far beyond a few moments.

Growing even more despairing but hoping to come upon something recognizable, Fabrizio raced down the corridor. Finding nothing familiar, he plunged down the first flight of steps he came to. Upon reaching a landing, he was quite sure he'd come to a place not very far from Mangus's room. Enormously relieved, he tore along the hallway, looking at all the doors, When he found theirs, he burst into the room.

Mangus was not there. Even more ominous, the magician's costume was nowhere in sight.

Fabrizio's agitation redoubled. Now, not only was he certain he had overslept, he was convinced Mangus had begun his performance at the ghostly niche, and he, upon whom so much depended, was not even close to where he should be.

His panic complete, Fabrizio tore out of the room and hurtled down the hallway. When he came upon steps he recognized, he plunged down two at a time, then tore along another hallway, made a turn — only to be confronted by soldiers guarding the way.

"Halt!" one of them cried.

Spinning about, Fabrizio flung himself down the hallway in the opposite direction. The soldiers began to chase after him.

Though Fabrizio ran fast, his pursuers were just as swift. So when he sped around a corner and spied a tapestry upon the wall that looked vaguely familiar, he decided to take a chance. He skidded to a stop and lifted a corner. Discovering a door behind it, he jerked it open, leaped through, and plunged back into complete darkness.

From within, he heard footsteps of running soldiers outside. Fearful of being caught, he charged blindly forward, tripping over something that sent him sprawling onto the floor. He leaped up and flung himself forward in an attempt to find a way out. When he discovered what felt like yet another door, he pulled it open and found himself in a new corridor. Not a soldier was in sight. Best of all, he recognized the area. He was close to the chapel.

Gasping for breath, he ran a few steps along the hall until he reached the chapel door. He pulled at it, only to find it closed. He yanked at it a few times, trying to get it open. Even as he did, he thought he heard a sound within. Summoning up all his strength, he hauled back on the door. With a snap, it came open. Someone must have latched it from inside. Not caring, Fabrizio jumped inside and shut the door behind him. In almost one leap he crossed the room and peered down through the green-tinted glass into the corridor below.

To his enormous relief, no one was there. What's more, everything he and Mangus had arranged was still in place. He was still early. All was not lost. His panic drained away.

Determined nonetheless to put everything in readiness, he turned about. Only then did he realize that the altar flame was out. Simultaneously he realized there were no candles in the chapel at all. Whirling, he turned to the large candelabra only to discover that the big candle — the one by which he was supposed to create the ghostly image — was entirely gone. Everything pertaining to the making of the ghostly light had been removed.

Stunned, Fabrizio stood in the middle of the chapel, trying to grasp the situation. He could barely think, much less make sense of the situation. Then he recalled that there were lamps alight in the hallways. He could get a flame from one of them.

He rushed to the door, pulled it open, and looked out. Soldiers were milling about at the far end of the corridor. Certain that they were searching for him, he retreated back into the chapel, where he could only hope they would not enter. Not wishing to be discovered, he scrambled back behind the altar to hide only to come to a dead stop. He gasped. Once again, somebody was on the floor.

It was Rinaldo, the kitchen boy.

The boy's clothing was torn in many places and streaked with blood. His face was marked with what also looked like blood. All around him were bits of broken candle. A sword was at his side. What's more, he was writhing about, clutching his left leg tightly. When he looked up at Fabrizio, tears were streaming from his eyes.

"What are you doing here!" Fabrizio demanded. "What have you done!"

"I . . . I hurt my leg," Rinaldo whimpered.

"But . . . but . . . you've ruined everything," Fabrizio cried. "The candles are all destroyed."

"I'm sorry. I'm terribly sorry. You must find a way."

"Find a way to do what?"

"To make the ghost."

"Who are you?" Fabrizio demanded. "How do you know about any of this?"

"Fabrizio," the boy said, "I am not Rinaldo, as I told you. I . . . I am Prince Lorenzo. Heir to the royal throne of Pergamontio."

"Prince Lorenzo!"

"You must believe me."

"But . . . but . . . ," Fabrizio gasped, "that's impossible. He's dead."

"I assure you, I am anything but dead. I was in the midst of destroying the candles when I heard you coming. I had no idea it was you. You're early. When you tried to get in, I ran to hide here, only to trip and strike my leg. It hurts terribly. I can't walk."

"But how could you be the prince?" Fabrizio demanded again. "I don't believe you."

"Listen quickly," Lorenzo said, speaking in an urgent whisper. "My mother and sister said they told you about my being sent to Rome with a guard appointed by Scarazoni. That was enough to make me uneasy and constantly on guard. When the man made a clumsy attempt upon my life, I thwarted him and forced him to reveal Scarazoni's plot.

"Scarazoni had paid the man to murder me and steal whatever valuables I had. He was to send my bloody garments to the castello as proof that I had been killed by bandits.

"I had the rogue imprisoned. Then I sent these very garments — rent and covered with chicken blood — to Scarazoni.

"In disguise, I made my way back to the castello and found employment in the kitchen. With my knowledge of the many secret passages, it was easy for my sister and I to meet. We included my mother in our plot, and the three of us met nightly here in the private chapel to make our plans."

Fabrizio suddenly remembered how surprised Mangus had been when the queen emerged from the cabinet. Had he thought it was going to be Lorenzo?

"But, why," Fabrizio asked, "could you not have just informed your father, the king, of what Scarazoni had done?"

"Fabrizio, what proof did we have? It would have been my word against Scarazoni's. We were not certain the king would believe in the count's treachery. And, if the king did not believe, the man would be free to strike again.

"So we three — my mother, sister, and I —

decided it would be better for me to stay hidden and act as we did."

"But why have you destroyed the candles?" Fabrizio wanted to know. "What have you gained by that?"

"Fabrizio, we were fearful our ghostly light would not be enough to frighten Scarazoni. We wanted to make the ghost as real as possible. I was going to crawl through the smoke that Mangus plans to make and stand up in the middle of the stage and pretend to be my own ghost." He indicated the sword. "If necessary, I was going to kill him. It's our best chance. We must succeed.

"The queen had retained my bloody garments. As you can see, I've put them on. But, Fabrizio, I can hardly stand." He grimaced with pain.

"Wait here!" Fabrizio urged, then tore back to the green windows and looked down. What he saw made his heart contract. Mangus, dressed in his magician robes and star-dangling cap, had arrived. As Fabrizio watched, he saw King Claudio, Queen Jovanna, Princess Teresina, as well as Count Scarazoni approach.

Mangus bowed to the newcomers. "With permission, my ladies, my lords," Fabrizio heard him say, "please be seated."

The king, queen, and princess sat. Count Scarazoni chose to stand behind the others.

Fabrizio rushed back to Lorenzo. "They've come," he whispered. "It's about to begin."

"But there will be no ghost!" Lorenzo moaned.

Fabrizio tried to help Lorenzo stand, but it was of little use. He was in too much pain.

"Lorenzo," Fabrizio said, "I have an idea."

"What?"

"I must be the ghost."

"You!" Lorenzo cried.

"Quickly! Or all is lost. Let me put on your bloody clothing, then make my way down there and become the ghost. It's our only chance to stop Scarazoni!"

Lorenzo stared openmouthed at Fabrizio. Then he said, "You are right!"

Frantic, the two boys exchanged clothing, Fabrizio taking Lorenzo's clothes and smearing his face with blood as well. As he dressed frantically, the prince told Fabrizio how to reach the corridor. "Will you remember?"

Fabrizio, his heart pounding madly, nodded.

"Here," Lorenzo said, "take my sword."

After a moment of hesitation, Fabrizio grasped it, then pushed his way into the cabinet. Hurrying, he came out the other side, peeked out into a hallway, saw that there were no soldiers, then darted across the way. Following the prince's instructions, he pushed upon a shield mounted on the wall. A door swung open, revealing a flight of steps that went down. Fabrizio stepped forward and pulled the door shut behind him. Once more, he was engulfed by darkness.

chapter 27

Fabrizio quickly reached the bottom of the steps. With a free hand he felt for the outline of a wooden door and found it quickly. Moving with caution, he pressed his weight against it. It creaked open. Then, with even greater care, he poked his head out and peeked down the corridor.

He could see Mangus. He was standing before the king and queen, as well as the princess. They were seated. Scarazoni — somewhat apart — was standing behind them.

As Fabrizio looked on, Mangus spoke slowly and with great solemnity. "My lords, my ladies," he began, "with permission, I ask you to be patient with me. I trust I will be successful this evening. But when dealing with the supernatural, one can never be sure what will occur. Something may happen. Or nothing may. Above all, I must ask — with permission — that you do not interfere. May I request that the princess come forward and stand before me."

Fabrizio watched Scarazoni. The count made a quick, nervous motion with his hand. "It may be so," he muttered.

Princess Teresina stood. Her hair was combed down the back of her simple white robe. She was very pale but composed. Her hands were clasped before her. She looked, Fabrizio thought, like an angel.

Mangus clasped his hands and bowed. Fabrizio was sure he was praying. Before he had concluded, the cathedral bells began to chime in the city below the castello. Twelve peals in all. It was midnight.

Fabrizio felt a shiver run through his body.

"Now then," Mangus said, "with permission, we shall begin." Moving slowly, burning candle in hand, he moved among his pots and jars and set them all alight.

Colored smoke began to billow, thick enough to hide walls, ceiling, and floor. Flames, both green and white, sputtered. Some candles burned slowly, while others sparkled. Now and again there came an unexpected *bang* as bits of gunpowder — embedded in some of the candles — burst into fire. The flags, with their mystic signs, fluttered. The smell of incense — cinnamon and sandalwood — was strong. The moaning jars produced a soft, undulating sound.

With grave demeanor and slow movement, Mangus took his position in the middle of his garden of flame, smoke, and scents. Once there, he closed his eyes, lifted his hands, and began to chant the nonsense words he had composed for the occasion.

Uxum, porabend, jaluba, whelf!
Uxum, porabend, jaluba, whelf!
By fetid frogs, and scummy snails,
Slithering snakes and rotting whales
And all ye lower creatures who
Creep beneath corrupted dew
In places rank and dark and deep!
I call on thee who wander in a restless sleep
Of painful and confus'd daze.

Release thyself from lost and weary ways!
Free thyself from death's hard chain!
For if thy grief is heartfelt pain
Visit with the living and now speak!
Free thyself from all thy reek
Uxum, porabend, jaluba, whelf!
Uxum, porabend, jaluba, whelf!

At the other end of the corridor, Fabrizio muttered a short prayer in hopes that there would be enough smoke to conceal him. Then, with Prince Lorenzo's sword held tightly in one hand, he dropped down to his knees and began to crawl forward beneath the clouds of smoke.

"Princess Teresina!" he heard Mangus exclaim. "I beg you to step forward. Allow yourself to be seen by eyes that can no longer see. Allow yourself to be spoken to by throats that no longer speak. Allow yourself to be touched by those who have lost all power to feel.

Uxum, porabend, jaluba, whelf!
Uxum, porabend, jaluba, whelf!

Fabrizio, the sound of his heart pounding in his ears, continued to crawl forward.

"Harken to us, spirits," he heard Mangus chant.

Candles exploded. The moaning seemed to be growing louder.

Mangus went on:

Speak out, ye perturbed ghosts!
All thee unfettered hosts
Come find your promised blessed sleep
By casting off your endless weep.
Pass through these clouds of graying mist.
Walk this earth where once you walked before!
Tell us of your pain, your gore,
Walk upon this living earth once more!

When Fabrizio drew as close as he dared to where Mangus was standing, the boy pulled himself into a kneeling position. The roiling, dense smoke stung his eyes so much, tears began to roll down his face. Only with effort did he keep from coughing. Mangus himself was enveloped in clouds of multicolored smoke so dense, Fabrizio kept losing sight of him.

Fabrizio edged forward only to bump against the platform. Horrified that he had given himself away, he froze.

As the smoke grew even thicker, and the moaning louder, Fabrizio heard Mangus call, "Come to us, spirit. Show us your being! *Now!*"

It was the signal for the ghost to appear, the moment for the glow to appear upon the wall.

Heart hammering, Fabrizio forced himself to stand up, then step onto the platform. Once secure, he moved forward, feeling for the platform's front edge with his feet in hopes he would not stumble.

Gradually, Fabrizio began to make out Mangus through the smoke. The old man was staring right at him, a look of astonishment on his face. It was as if he could not believe what he himself was seeing.

Fabrizio edged forward. Now he began to see the king, the queen, and the princess across the way. Then Scarazoni came into view.

The king leaped to his feet. "It's there!" he cried. "I see it!" The others leaned forward to see.

Mangus lifted his hands high and continued to speak in his exalted tones. But there was a hesitancy in his voice that Fabrizio had never heard before. "Come to us . . . unhappy spirit. Be generous in your grief. Show us . . . your wounds! Bring us the truth of your . . . pain."

Now it was the princess who shouted, "It's Lorenzo! He has returned!"

"It's my son!" the queen cried.

The princess held her hands up toward the ghost as though imploring it.

The queen was standing, staring. So, too, was the king. Count Scarazoni pushed himself back against the far wall, as if trying to keep his distance. As he gazed at the ghostly figure, his eyes were wide and full of fear.

Mangus stepped forward, staring into the clouds of smoke as if trying to see just what it was that was before him. Suddenly, Fabrizio thought he detected a momentary smile. But it was gone as quickly as it had come. The next moment, Mangus stood tall and cried, "Oh, ghost, I see your head, arms, fingers and torso. Your clothing is torn and cut in many places. You have bloodstains everywhere. Your decayed body is spotted with gore. Your hair is in disarray. You have pushed your way through the corrupt netherworld.

"Spirit," Mangus called again. "Uxum, porabend, jaluba, whelf! Will you, can you, speak to us!"

"Yes . . . I . . . will . . . speak," Fabrizio called out in a slow, stuttering voice, speaking so low, his chin was touching his chest.

"What do you want of me?" the princess replied. "Why have you haunted me?"

"Revenge . . . ," Fabrizio said. *"Revenge."*

"Revenge for what?" Mangus asked.

"For . . . a . . . wrongful . . . death."

"Whose wrongful death?"

"My . . . *murder!*" Fabrizio shrieked. "For I am the ghost of Prince Lorenzo. . . ."

"Stop him!" Count Scarazoni abruptly shouted. "It is a fraud! Mangus is no magician. It's all a hoax! A fraud!"

The king whirled about. In his hand was his unsheathed dagger. He pointed it right at Scarazoni. "Silence!" he shouted. Over his shoulder he cried, "Speak to the spirit, Teresina. Speak to it before it goes!"

"Spirit, how did my brother die?" Teresina cried out.

Fabrizio shifted first one way and then another, as if in search of someone. Suddenly, over his head, a bolt of lightning crackled. Taken by surprise, the boy started. Even Mangus jumped.

Quickly recovering, Fabrizio lifted his arm and pointed across the corridor, right at

Scarazoni. "Lord . . . Scarazoni . . . planned . . . it," he said in as ghostly a voice as he could manage. "Signore Addetto . . . gave the count the idea. The count seeks . . . the royal title. It is Scarazoni . . . who . . . is . . . the traitor."

"Liar!" Scarazoni shouted. "Mangus is no magician. This is a fraud! A hoax!"

But the king had backed him up against the wall. "Guards to the rescue!" the king cried. "Guards to the rescue!"

Almost immediately, armed soldiers came pouring down the corridor and into the area.

"Seize him!" the king cried.

The soldiers hesitated.

"I am your commander," Scarazoni shouted. "I am the new king!"

In a great rage, the true king shouted, "Treason! Arrest him!"

At that, Count Scarazoni burst forward, butting the king away and storming past the soldiers. The queen, too, was shoved to one side. Teresina turned and screamed while Mangus looked on with amazement.

Scarazoni, sword in hand, drove toward Fabrizio as though prepared to run him through.

Fabrizio, using all his willpower to keep from bolting, stepped nervously out of the smoke.

"Scarazoni!" he cried out in a voice wavering with fear. "Behold the one you had murdered. Behold your victim! I am he!"

It was too much for Scarazoni. He stopped short and stared, openmouthed, at the figure before him. Fabrizio's tears — brought on by the smoke — were washing away the stain on his face so that it appeared as if his face were dripping blood.

"Confess your crimes," Fabrizio cried, "or I shall slay you now!" So saying, his trembling arms lifted up his sword and made as if to strike.

Scarazoni became paralyzed with terror.

When Fabrizio took another step forward, the count let his sword drop upon the stone floor with an empty clatter. Then he fell to his knees.

"Confess!" Fabrizio cried excitedly. "Confess!"

"I . . . do . . . I . . . do," Scarazoni whimpered. "I did order the murder of the prince. I did kill Addetto. I admit to it all! Send him away, Mangus! Send him away."

As the smoke began to roll away, the king came forward and, with the handle of his sword, struck Scarazoni down. "Take him away," he cried. "Take him away!"

This time, the soldiers obeyed. A weeping Scarazoni was led down the corridor.

Fabrizio remained in place.

As the smoke evaporated, it was left to Mangus to cry out, "Bravo! Fabrizio! Bravo! A wonderful performance. But, you rascal, how did you ever get here?"

chapter 28

The next day, Mangus and Fabrizio were brought before the king in open court. So many courtiers were there, the great room seemed like a bubbling pot of color and fashion.

Before the multitude of lords and ladies, the king declared Count Scarazoni a traitor and that when the week was out, he would have his fair trial and then be executed.

Then he proclaimed Mangus a dear friend of his reign and freed him from all constraints upon his life and liberty. (In private, however, he had already warned Mangus not to go back to magician's ways. Mangus was only too happy to foreswear such a life and devote himself to his pursuit of truth and reason.)

The queen then spoke loudly about how Mangus had helped to restore her son, the prince, to his proper home and place. And, indeed, when Prince Lorenzo spoke — dressed in such finery, Fabrizio found it difficult to recognize the kitchen boy — it was to bestow upon Mangus a pension that would last the old man the rest of his life.

Then it was the turn of Princess Teresina to stand and publicly thank Fabrizio for *his* heroism, pronounce him a citizen, give him the freedom of the Kingdom of Pergamontio, and present him with a reward of fifty gold lira. Finally she asked him if he would be her servant.

Fabrizio, in a new suit of clothing, stepped forward, bowed low, and said, "My lady, with permission, I must decline your kind offer. It is to my master, Mangus, to whom I owe my loyalty. You know what people say, 'An old leather shoe gives the traveler more comfort than a new shoe of gold.'"

Shortly thereafter, Mangus and Fabrizio were placed in one of the king's carriages to be carried home in triumph. This time the insignia was showing, and the windows were open.

As they went home, Mangus and Fabrizio talked about all that had been done. Fabrizio praised the magician for his effective performance.

"Perhaps," Mangus returned. "But it was my last piece of theater. It was all too real. When I began to perceive a form in the middle of the smoke, there was a moment when I was . . . well, puzzled."

Fabrizio grinned. "Master, I saw that moment. With permission, did you think I was a real ghost?"

"Not even for a moment," Mangus insisted, though he smiled as he spoke.

"Now, Master," Fabrizio said, "with permission, there was one thing you did that I had never seen you do before."

"And that was?"

"The lightning over my head."

"You are still teasing me, Fabrizio. That lightning was none of my making. Indeed, I was about to ask you how you did that."

Fabrizio considered Mangus for a long moment. "Master," he finally said, "you know what they say, 'Being small allows one to have large secrets.'"

Mangus, content with the answer, laughed.

Fabrizio stared out the window.

That night, since it was no longer necessary

to sleep in the front hallway, Fabrizio retired to his tiny attic room at the top of Mangus's house. Once again, the tarot cards lay before him. Once again, he waited until he heard the cathedral bells ring twelve times. At the stroke of midnight, he flipped over the first card. It was

THE SERVANT

Smiling broadly, Fabrizio turned the next card. . . .

about the author

A vi is the author of over thirty-five books for children and teenagers, and it is a measure of his extraordinary popularity with young readers that nearly every one of his books remains in print. His work encompasses an impressive array of genres, including historical fiction, short stories, a documentary novel, a picture book, sports fiction, animal stories, fantasy, coming-of-age, a novel told all in dialogue, and of course stories of ghostly adventure like *Midnight Magic*.

Among Avi's many awards are two Newbery Honor Book citations, the Christopher Medal, and the *Boston Globe/Horn Book* Award; his books have also been voted onto many children's choice and state master reading lists.

Midnight Magic is Avi's second book for Scholastic Press. His first, *Perloo the Bold,* was praised as "an exciting, suspenseful, and witty tale of conspiracy" (*Publishers Weekly,* starred review). *VOYA* called it "a fast-paced, compelling read that will keep young readers turning the pages," and the *Horn Book* cited its "theatrical dialogue, good guys (and a girl) to root for, a high-minded but firm-footed theme, and tons of action."

Formerly a librarian, Avi is now a full-time writer. He makes his home in Denver, Colorado.